"The only way to handle you, my dear, is to tame you."

"Tame me?" Molly jerked out of Samuel's grasp. "Tame me!" She stalked up and down the hallway, then whirled around and faced him. "I'd just like to see you try!"

He leaned nonchalantly against the doorjamb and smiled at her...not a smile of mirth...but the cold, deadly smile of a man about to go into battle.

"I'd advise you not to issue challenges, my dear. I find them impossible to resist."

"That's not all you're liable to find impossible to resist before this is over." Molly put her hands on her hips. Her color was high, and her eyes sparkled with wrath.

"Anger becomes you, Venus."

She gave a mock bow. "Thank you, Sir Adams The Bold."

"Don't thank me yet." He moved slowly toward her, pinning her to the spot with his hot, dark eyes. "But you can come closer. I find it impossible to tame a woman who's halfway across the room."

Dear Reader:

Happy July! It's a month for warm summer evenings, barbecues and—of course—the Fourth of July. It's a time of enjoyment and family gatherings. It's a time for romance!

The fireworks are sparkling this month at Silhouette Romance. Our DIAMOND JUBILEE title is *Borrowed Baby* by Marie Ferrarella, a heartwarming story about a brooding loner who suddenly becomes a father when his sister leaves him with a little bundle of joy! Then, next month, don't miss *Virgin Territory* by Suzanne Carey. Dedicated bachelor Phil Catterini is determined to protect the virtue of Crista O'Malley—and she's just as determined to change her status as "the last virgin in Chicago." Looks like his bachelorhood will need the protection instead as these two lovers go hand in hand into virgin territory.

The DIAMOND JUBILEE—Silhouette Romance's tenth anniversary celebration—is our way of saying thanks to you, our readers. To symbolize the timelessness of love, as well as the modern gift of the tenth anniversary, we're presenting readers with a DIAMOND JUBILEE Silhouette Romance title each month, penned by one of your favorite Silhouette Romance authors. In the coming months, writers such as Annette Broadrick, Lucy Gordon, Dixie Browning and Phyllis Halldorson are writing DIAMOND JUBILEE titles especially for you.

And that's not all! There are six books a month from Silhouette Romance—stories by wonderful authors who time and time again bring home the magic of love. During our anniversary year, each book is special and written with romance in mind. July brings you *Venus de Molly* by Peggy Webb—a sequel to her heartwarming *Harvey's Missing*. The second book in Laurie Paige's poignant duo, *Homeward Bound*, is coming your way in July. Don't miss *Home Fires Burning Bright*—Carson and Tess's story. And much-loved Diana Palmer has some special treats in store in the month ahead. Don't miss Diana's fortieth Silhouette—*Connal*. He's a LONG, TALL TEXAN out to lasso your heart, and he'll be available in August....

I hope you'll enjoy this book and all of the stories to come. Come home to romance—Silhouette Romance—for always!

Sincerely,

Tara Hughes Gavin
Senior Editor

PEGGY WEBB

Venus de Molly

Silhouette Romance

Published by Silhouette Books New York

America's Publisher of Contemporary Romance

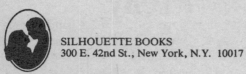

SILHOUETTE BOOKS
300 E. 42nd St., New York, N.Y. 10017

Copyright © 1990 by Peggy Webb

ISBN: 0-373-08735-7

First Silhouette Books printing July 1990

Printed in the U.S.A.

Books by Peggy Webb

Silhouette Romance

When Joanna Smiles #645
A Gift for Tenderness #681
Harvey's Missing #712
Venus de Molly #735

PEGGY WEBB

grew up in a large northeastern Mississippi family where the Southern tradition of storytelling was elevated to an art. "In our family there was always a romance or a divorce or a scandal going on," she says, "and always someone willing to tell it. By the time I was thirteen I knew I would be a writer."

Over the years Peggy has raised her two children—and twenty-five dogs. "Any old stray is welcome," she acknowledges. "My house is known as Dog Heaven." Recently her penchant for trying new things led her to take karate lessons. Although she was the oldest person in her class and one of only two women, she now has a blue belt in Tansai Karate. Her karate hobby came to a halt, though, when wrens built a nest in her punching bag. "I decided to take up bird-watching," says Peggy.

MISSISSIPPI AND ALABAMA

Prologue

Mother, this is a foolish thing to do."

Glory Ethel Adams leaned back in the comfortable chair and gazed around the opulent office; then she looked at her son. He was sitting behind his big impressive desk, wearing an immaculate three-piece suit and the composed look of a man completely in charge. Her Sammy was a fine figure of a man: tall, handsome and well built, with the black hair and eyes of his daddy. He was smart, too. President of the bank and on every board that was worth being on in Florence. The governor of Alabama even consulted Samuel Adams on financial matters.

There was no doubt about it, Samuel was a powerful man . . . and a son to be proud of. But she did wish, just this once, he'd remember that family didn't need so much bossing and telling what to do.

She shifted in her chair and fanned herself with the letter in her hand. It was hotter than usual this summer, and it made her wish she'd lost that fifteen pounds she'd been planning to lose since last November. But it was too late for that now.

Rising from her chair, she smoothed out the letter and placed it on her son's desk.

"Just read the letter, Sam. It might change your mind."

Samuel didn't usually lose patience with his mother, or with anybody else for that matter, but this business of marrying a man she had met through a lonely-hearts club was enough to make a saint curse.

He shoved the letter aside.

"I know all I need to know about Jedidiah Rakestraw. He's some old codger who is clever enough to take advantage of a lonely divorcée with money."

Glory Ethel burst out laughing.

"I don't see a damned thing funny about that."

"What's so funny is that I've never had a lonely day in my life, and I don't give a hoot in a fiddle about the money. I'd give it all to the first beggar who came along if you didn't have it tucked away in *safe* investments."

His mother was impossible. That's all there was to it. Impatiently, Samuel picked up the letter and scanned its contents. It was even worse than he expected.

Folding the letter into a neat rectangle, he stood up and came around the desk. Maybe he could reason with her.

"He sounds educated enough, I'll grant you that."

"See? Didn't I tell you?"

"It's not intellectual stimulation I'm worried about; it's his family. Just listen to this." He reopened the letter and began to read selected passages. "'You'll love my daughter. She's something of a hellion—a woman after your own heart, if I'm not mistaken. She went off to

Paris to study art and ended up being an artist's model. I expect every art collector who is anybody knows about the famous nude statue *Venus de Molly*'.... Venus de Molly!" He lifted one sardonic eyebrow to show what he thought of that.

"I think it's cute, Sam."

"What I think won't do to tell in polite society."

Glory Ethel chuckled. "It's not the end of the world."

No, he thought. It was just the end of everything he'd worked for these last twenty years—rebuilding the family fortune and the family name. Venus de Molly. Good Lord!

He studied his mother. He didn't want to hurt her; all he wanted to do was convince her not to make a foolish mistake. Briefly he consulted the letter again, looking for arguments to win his case.

"And if that scandalous daughter isn't enough, there are his friends. What kind of man has friends who have a double wedding with their dogs... and serve an Alpo wedding cake at the reception?"

"A lively man. And I intend to marry him." Ethel stood and smoothed down the front of her seersucker dress, then picked up her purse, the hefty summer straw bag that held everything from lipstick, which she seldom used, to a dog-eared copy of *The Canterbury Tales*, which she did use. Sometimes she fancied herself to be the Wife of Bath.

Samuel knew that stubborn look on her face. He tried one last ploy.

"There's no telling what impact this man will have on us. His daughter is a nude model. We don't need another scandal in the family. Just think about it awhile longer."

"I'm seventy-three years old. I don't have much time left to think." She patted her son's cheek. "Sam, you're a smart man and I respect your opinion, but I've never taken orders from my children, and I don't intend to start now. I'm going to marry Jedidiah Rakestraw. And there's not a damned thing you can do about it."

"He's already got you cussing."

"That's not all he's liable to do. I might even take up gambling and lying and heavy petting."

"Good Lord, Mother! Can't you be serious? You don't even know this man."

"Yes, I do. He came to Florence last month for the specific purpose of getting to know me. And if you weren't so all-fired stubborn, you'd know him, too. He wanted to meet you."

"I had a business meeting in Montgomery."

Glory Ethel relented a little. After all, it wasn't Sam's fault that he was so bossy. He'd had to be the man in the family since he was fifteen. She patted his stern face once more. "Sammy...Sammy. Come with me to Tupelo. Jedidiah and I want our children to get to know each other before the wedding."

"I can't think of a single reason I'd want to know a woman who gets paid for taking off her clothes."

"For starters, she's going to be a member of the family."

Not if he had anything to do about it. But he knew better than to tell his mother that. His legendary stubbornness was inherited from her.

"I'm going to Tupelo with you, but this doesn't mean I've changed my mind about the Rakestraws. I'm going to take care of you and to watch after the family's interests."

Glory Ethel smiled. Sam was a dictator, but he was a benevolent and reasonable one. She was counting on the Rakestraws to change his mind . . . especially Molly. Venus de Molly. How intriguing.

Samuel kept one eye on his mother as he picked up the phone to make arrangements with the Rakestraws. He knew that self-satisfied smile on her face. It meant nothing but trouble.

Chapter One

Molly Rakestraw loved gardening.

She straightened from the flower bed where she had been planting a row of bright red petunias. She knew it was a little late in the season for planting, but she'd only found this lovely old house on Robins Street for Papa last week, and she wanted to do everything she could to make it bright and cheerful and homey before his fiancée arrived. Glory Ethel Adams. What a name! Molly loved her already.

She wiped her sweaty face with the back of her hand and leaned over to give Papa's two dogs a hug—Mickey and Minnie, offspring of Harvey, a big lovable stray, and Gwendolyn, his pedigreed poodle "wife," who were owned by Dan and Janet Albany, Papa's best friends.

Molly released the dogs and sat back on her heels to survey her work. The petunias looked a little wilted, but a good spraying with water would help that. She turned on the faucet and picked up the hose. The petunias perked up under the sprinkle, and so did Mickey and Minnie. Somehow, watering the flowers became a circus, with Molly as ringleader. That wasn't unusual. Most things she did usually turned into a celebration of some kind.

She cavorted with the dogs, spraying them and herself with equal enthusiasm. There was so much laughter and barking that she didn't hear the car pull up in Papa's driveway.

"Excuse me."

The voice, coming so unexpectedly, startled her. Molly whirled around, the hose still in her hand. Water spattered on her visitor's polished black shoes and soaked the pants of his immaculate three-piece suit.

He jumped back out of firing range.

"I'm so sorry." Still dragging the hose with her, Molly leaned down and swiped at the water on his shoes. The hose nozzle got out of hand and shot a stream of water straight up into his face. "Oh, dear." Molly stood to correct her mistake and sent a stream of water cascading down the front of his shirt. "I *do* apologize."

"My dear, if you apologize anymore I'm likely to drown." The stranger lifted the hose out of her hand and twisted the nozzle shut.

Molly stepped back to survey the stranger. Being soaking wet didn't keep him from being the most delicious-looking man she'd ever seen. In fact it only enhanced his charms. She couldn't imagine, though, why anybody would be wearing such a ridiculous outfit on such a hot and steamy day. He had to be an insurance salesman; they were always out to impress.

"You must be Molly," he said.

She was pleased that he knew her name. She'd been back in Tupelo only three weeks now, but she did love fame and notoriety. She supposed that by now everybody in the city knew that Venus de Molly was back in town.

She smiled and extended her hand. "Molly Rakestraw. And you must be..."

"Samuel Adams." He looked askance at the grubby hand she held out, hesitated a second and then took it cautiously, as if he expected to become contaminated by the dirt.

Out of perverseness, she gave his hand a hard squeeze and hung on long enough to transfer a good portion of gardening soil to him. He looked like the kind of man who would benefit from getting dirty every now and then.

"My goodness, I didn't expect you until Tuesday."

"This *is* Tuesday."

She tossed her head in a way that set her golden braid a-swing and all her jewelry a-tinkle. "I would have sworn it was Saturday. But then time means nothing to me. I think one day is just as delightful as the next, don't you?"

He lifted one eyebrow. "I've never thought about it."

Molly looked him up and down once again. For all his delicious looks, he was as remote and formidable as an arctic glacier at high noon. Her heart sank. Good Lord, if Glory Ethel was anything like her son, Papa would be miserable. He needed a lively woman, not some ice-encased autocrat. She'd have to do something about that.

"Just listen to me, standing here chattering while you're dripping wet. Where's your mother?"

"In the car."

"Gracious, in this heat?"

"I left the motor running and the air-conditioning on so she would be cool while I checked to see if we had the right house."

He was exactly the type who would do something practical and sensible like that. She would have bailed out, bags and all, dragging Papa by the hand and calling to everybody that she had arrived.

"Please bring her in. Papa is eager to see her again, and I can't wait to meet her."

"Will you excuse me while I go and get her?"

"Certainly."

Molly waited in the yard while Samuel Adams went to get his mother.

Water swished in his shoes and drizzled down his legs. What was more, his right hand looked as if he had been down in the dirt making mud cakes. Molly Rakestraw was even worse than he had expected. He dreaded meeting the father. Anyone who would raise such a Bohemian daughter had to have a few screws loose somewhere.

He was close to cursing by the time he reached his car. Bending down, he opened the door and got inside. For once it didn't matter that he was dripping water and dirt all over the leather seats of his Rolls-Royce Silver Cloud. There were more important considerations.

"What in the world . . ." Glory Ethel was already grasping the door handle in order to get out.

"Just please be quiet a minute and listen to me, Mother."

"I'm listening."

"The best thing we can do right now is turn around and head back to Florence. I've met the daughter, and I can tell you that if her father is anything like that, you don't want to be within a city block of him."

"Was that Molly you were talking to?"

"Yes."

"She's gorgeous."

"How could you tell under all that dirt and jewelry? She must be wearing five pounds of turquoise and silver. To garden in, for gosh sakes. And I've never seen a woman bare more flesh than that outside the bedroom." He paused to loosen his tie.

Glory Ethel laughed. "I see she got to you."

"This is not one of Chaucer's bawdy tales; this is real life. It's not the woman that is bothering me; it's the heat."

Glory Ethel turned and stared out the window. Molly was still in the yard, cavorting with two dogs.

"She is the most stunning woman I've ever seen, and if she likes me I'm liable to marry Jedidiah on the spot." She turned around and grinned at her son. "Are you going to escort me like the perfect gentleman you are, or am I going to have to get out of this car and go visit the Rakestraws all by myself?"

Samuel knew that mood. Right now it was useless to argue with his mother. He'd make the best of the situation and save his arguments for later.

"Mother, you're giving me ulcers."

"I wish you'd give *me* something."

"What?"

"Grandchildren."

He'd heard that before. And so had Beatrice, his sister. Steeling himself for another encounter with Venus de Molly, Samuel got out of the car. He was determined to see this through. As he helped Glory Ethel from the car, he glanced at the woman in the yard. She was bending over her dogs with her back to him. She had the most astonishing legs he'd ever seen. They were long and tanned and extraordinarily beautiful. Perfect. The word came to his mind just as Molly straightened and turned to smile at him. Good grief. Everything about her was perfect: the wide turquoise eyes, the flawless skin, the high cheekbones, the generous mouth, the exquisitely proportioned body. No wonder artists and sculptors wanted her for a model.

He could imagine the havoc a woman like that would wreak in his carefully ordered world. There were men in Florence who would fight for just a glimpse of her. And his mother wanted her to be part of the family! All the years he'd spent rebuilding the family respectability would be for nothing.

"Are you going to stare at her all day, or are you going to take me in to meet this girl?"

He jerked his attention back to his mother. "I wasn't staring."

Glory Ethel merely gave him a secret smile and urged him up the yard to meet Molly.

His mother had never met a person she didn't like, and Molly was no exception. Glory Ethel greeted her with a huge hug, mindless of the dirt and water she got on the front of her dress.

"My dear, I can't tell you how I've looked forward to meeting Jedidiah's daughter. You're even more beautiful than I imagined you would be."

Samuel could tell the compliment pleased Molly. Her smile was absolutely radiant. He'd known women like that—all surface and no substance. They had no appeal for him whatsoever. Ignoring the dazzle of that smile, he concentrated on her shortcomings. Molly Rakestraw was obviously a frivolous, gullible woman who would believe anything a person told her if it were prefaced by a compliment. And gaudy. Good Lord! She was as gaudy as that floozy his father had run off with—that two-bit country singer who had come to cut a record at The Shoals and had ended up with all the Adams's family jewels, half the Adams fortune, and Taylor Adams to boot.

While he was tallying up Molly's faults, a slender distinguished-looking man came out the front door. He was a handsome older gentleman with a thick shock of silver hair and the bold nose and chin of a Roman gladiator. It was easy to see where Molly had gotten her good looks.

His mother fluttered and flirted like a schoolgirl. He didn't know how she finally managed to make the introductions.

Mr. Rakestraw gave Samuel's hand a firm shake and then turned his attention to Glory Ethel. Bending gallantly from the waist, he kissed her hand. "My dear, I've waited so long for this." He tucked her hand into the crook of his elbow. "While the children are getting acquainted, we'll go inside. I've made lemonade."

"That sounds lovely, Jedidiah." Glory Ethel cast a smile over her shoulder at her son and allowed herself to be escorted inside.

Samuel started to follow them and then he remembered his wet clothes. He hesitated, torn between wanting to keep an eye on his mother and not wanting to track mud into the house. His glance swung to Molly. Being stuck in the yard with her had all the appeal of jumping into a blender full of whipped cream and cherries. Southern manners and muddy shoes be hanged, he thought. He was going inside so he could keep his mother from making any more foolhardy mistakes.

He started toward the front door.

Molly reached out and caught his sleeve with one hand—the muddy one. But hell, what did a little more mud matter? He was already wearing enough to furnish his sister Bea with mud facials for a month or two.

He glanced down at the hand on his arm and lifted one eyebrow. His look of disapproval had been known to make people quake in their boots. Molly simply smiled at him.

"Why don't we sit outside? There's a lovely chinaberry tree beside the house."

The last thing in the world he wanted to do was sit under a chinaberry tree with Molly Rakestraw. He already knew more about her than he cared to. He started to decline, and then thought better of it. Maybe he could find out exactly what the Rakestraws were up to.

"Perhaps I can dry out a little while I sit under the...chinaberry, did you say?"

"Yes."

"You don't hear of many of those trees anymore."

Molly led the way to the swing, talking as she went. "I remember a great big old chinaberry tree on the farm where Papa grew up. In the summertime I used to pick the berries and pelt the neighborhood hoodlums who came over to bother the cat. We called her Miss Praline. She was exactly the color of a sugar praline."

"The boys must have had a hard time of it. I can vouch for your aim." He lifted his limp tie and squeezed water from it.

"I *am* sorry about your suit." She sized him up. "I'd offer you some of Papa's clothes, but I'm afraid they'd be too small."

"These are fine." He watched Molly as she sat down. Studying his opponent—that's what he was doing. It always worked in business. She smiled up at him, and the sun caught her eyes. They were brilliant turquoise. None of his opponents ever had eyes like that. But he was far too smart and worldly-wise to be taken in by a pair of hypnotic eyes.

He sat down and stretched his long legs out in front of him. It was impossible not to relax in a slatted swing. He'd allow his body to relax, but not his mind.

He gave Molly his best president-of-the-bank look. "Tell me about your father."

"He's a wonderful man, an open-minded freethinker whose world is not limited by rules and convention."

That's exactly what Samuel had thought. A muscle began to twitch in the side of his jaw.

"What else?"

His clipped tone and the disapproval in his face immediately got Molly's dander up. Somewhere in her family tree was an Irishman known for his fighting spirit. Whatever else had been watered down over the years, the fighting Irish had been left intact.

"Are you asking because you are interested or because you're trying to find some fatal flaw?"

For all her frivolous looks, she was smarter then he'd thought. It wouldn't do to underestimate his opponent. He sought to remedy the situation.

"Well, naturally I'm interested. I left important work in Florence to drive over and meet him."

"And I left important work in Paris to meet your mother. But you don't see me giving you the third degree about her. If she suits Papa, she's good enough for me."

"Naked modeling."

"What?"

"I said, naked modeling. Isn't that the *important* work you left in Paris?"

Molly's fist instinctively doubled, and only her good upbringing kept her from knocking him out of the swing. He'd pronounced "naked modeling" as if it were one of the seven deadly sins. Not only was he bossy, he was also judgmental. The Lord deliver her from a man who thought he knew everything.

"I guess it's the three-piece suit that gives you such a narrow view of life."

"I beg your pardon?"

"That tie is bound to cut off circulation to your brain, otherwise you would know the difference between naked and nude."

"It all boils down to the same thing. You pose without your clothes on," he told her.

"The human body is not sinful."

"I never said it was . . . in the right place."

"The bedroom, you mean?"

"Precisely."

"What I do is art, Mr. Adams, not sin."

"Labels don't change the facts. You bare yourself for the entire world to see, and you show absolutely no remorse."

Molly gave him another long, frank appraisal. Even in the wet crumpled suit, he was still a gorgeous man. But he was also a dictator, and she knew exactly how to deal with them. "I'm sorry about only one thing, Mr. Adams."

"What's that, Miss Rakestraw?"

"That I didn't drown you with the water hose when I had my chance." She put one foot on the ground and set the swing into gentle motion. Then she gave him a wicked grin. "And you can call me Molly."

"I can't think of one good reason why I should."

"Because, Samuel, my dear boy, it appears that we're going to be one big happy family." She gave him a big wink.

"Over my dead body."

"That can be arranged."

He boldly assessed her. In the space of twenty minutes she had made him forget manners, subtlety and reason. She was absolutely the most exasperating woman he'd ever met. The best he could hope for if his mother decided to go on with this foolishness would be to tame Molly enough to make her suitable for polite society.

Molly stared back. She'd never met a man she couldn't win with wit and charm. And yet, in less than an hour, this outrageous man had her acting like some angry alley cat on a hot tin roof. He was absolutely the most aggravating man she'd ever met. The best she could do if Papa decided to go ahead with the marriage would be to give this man his comeuppance. She'd never seen a man who needed it more desperately.

Inside the house, Jedidiah and Glory Ethel looked out the window at their children.

"Just look at them," he said, lifting his glass of lemonade for a leisurely sip, "out there swinging together like lifelong friends."

Glory Ethel smiled fondly at him. "It does the heart good to see our children getting along so well together."

"They certainly have taken a shine to each other." He leaned over and squeezed Glory Ethel's hand. "I'm happy to see things going so smoothly, my dear."

"So am I. Why don't we go outside and tell them our good news?"

They left their glasses on a silver tray and started toward the door. Halfway across the den, they got sidetracked by Jedidiah's collection of 1930s records, and before they knew it, they were listening to Glenn Miller's "String of Pearls" and holding hands.

Chapter Two

A warm summer breeze stirred the leaves of the chinaberry tree, setting a low-hanging limb into motion and loosening an overripe berry. The small golden fruit broke loose from its anchor and tumbled toward the swing. It landed with a soft plop on the front of Samuel Adams's white shirt.

It was the final straw. He quirked his eyebrow as if indicating it was all Molly's fault, and impatiently brushed away the offending berry.

She stifled her laughter. *It served him right.* She wished she'd thought of pelting him with berries herself. A good chinaberry war might loosen him up. She almost reached up and got a handful of berries, but she quickly changed her mind. After all, he *was* going to be a member of the family. She'd best try to make peace.

She scooted across the swing and leaned toward him. Up close, his eyes were startlingly black. They almost made her forget what she was doing.

"Here. Let me look at that." She plucked the front of his shirt between her thumb and forefinger. She felt his muscles quiver. At least she thought she did, but when she glanced at his face, he seemed perfectly in control. Her mind must be playing tricks.

"What are you doing?"

"Chinaberries are notorious for staining clothes, especially white shirts. I'm checking you out."

"You already did that—with the water hose."

Molly noticed the briefest flash of humor in his dark eyes. It almost redeemed him. She brushed at the berry stain again. Underneath his white shirt, Samuel Adams was solid muscle. She'd thought businessmen in three-piece suits would be soft and out of shape.

"I promise—no water hose this time."

"I'm not sure I can trust you."

"Most people do."

"The first thing you should know about me is that I am not like most people."

"Am I supposed to be scared? Or should I merely bow and kiss your feet?"

"I'd settle for a little bowing and foot kissing."

She almost caught him in a smile; almost but not quite. What would it take to loosen up this arrogant tyrant? She decided to try sneaky tactics.

Leaning closer she affected a flirtatious pout. "I much prefer the other kind." She circled her hand intimately across the front of his shirt.

From the looks of that poker face, she'd have thought he was entirely unaffected. But *this* time she knew better. Beneath her hand, his heart quickened its pace. She gave him a smile of pure female satisfaction.

He didn't trust that smile. "The other kind of what?"

"Kissing." Without warning, she leaned down and kissed his chest, right over his heart, right through his wet shirt.

He was so surprised he nearly fell out of the swing. He'd known many women in his lifetime, but he'd never known anyone quite like Molly. He looked down into those brilliant turquoise eyes in that perfectly sculpted face. Stubbornness. That's what he saw. Molly Rakestraw was a stubborn woman from top to bottom—from those pert little ears, all the way down to her muddy toes. He glanced at her feet again and did a double take. Good Lord. She was wearing gold snake sandals. The snake's head pointed between her toes and its tail curved halfway up her leg.

Molly was accustomed to being studied by men. She leaned back in the swing to enjoy Samuel's perusal.

"Do you like what you see?"

He quirked one eyebrow upward. "I don't like anything about you."

"Except the kiss. You enjoyed that."

"Don't get your hopes up."

Without ceremony, he plucked her hand off his chest and put it back into her lap. Giving it a fatherly pat, he winked at her.

"There's no need for us to get chummy," he continued. She seemed totally undisturbed by his lack of interest. He wanted to bother her a little, just enough to keep her off guard and give himself time to regain the upper hand. He played his trump card. "Besides, I'm not interested in teenagers."

"Teenagers!" She straightened so abruptly she almost fell off the swing. With her back as stiff as a cardboard Indian in a drugstore window and her eyes shooting fire, she glared at him. "I'll have you know I'm a woman—*all* woman."

He leaned back in the swing and subjected her to a long, lazy inspection. "I don't know," he drawled. "It could all be padding."

She was speechless for two seconds, and then she threw back her head and roared with uninhibited delight.

Now it was his turn to be speechless—but only for a moment.

"I don't see a damned thing funny about that."

She leaned back in the swing now, posing against the slats. It was impossible not to look, and hard not to be impressed. None of what he saw was padding, he'd guarantee it. But he didn't say so. He merely continued to study her as if she were a whipped-cream confection that he considered too sweet for his taste.

"The funny thing is that I'm twenty-three, which is a little long in the tooth for a model. As for the padding—you'll just have to take my word. I don't take off my clothes unless I'm paid an awful lot of money and unless the person asking says 'pretty please.'"

She studied him to see how he took that little white lie. Darn his hide! He was still as cool as snow in July.

"I don't recall asking."

"It's just as well, Samuel. I wouldn't have obliged, anyway." She leaned across the swing to pat his knee and to see if she could rattle him. "You don't mind if I call you 'Samuel,' do you, since we're going to be in the same family and all?"

"You can call my anything you like. Just know that I won't come when you call."

"That might be a refreshing change."

"You're accustomed to men doing your bidding? Is
that what you want me to think?"

She grinned at him again. "How do I know what *old*
men think."

"Old men?"

Her hand was still on his knee, and much to his surprise it was bothering him. He blamed it on overactive
hormones and having been too long without a woman.
His father had made a fool of himself over just such a
woman as Molly, and he wasn't about to repeat the mistakes of Taylor Adams.

"Yes. You must be at least forty-five."

It galled him that she had overestimated his age by ten
years. His mother was always telling him that he worked
too hard, but he didn't know it showed.

"That's experience showing. Bank presidents are
never teenagers."

"You're president of a bank?"

"Surely you knew that. Or perhaps only your father
did. But don't let it put any ideas into your pretty little
head."

Molly was torn between anger and laughter. By
George, he thought they were after his money. And that
crack about her "pretty little head" stung. He acted as
if a pretty woman didn't have the brains of a rabbit. If
ever a man deserved his comeuppance, it was Samuel
Adams. And she vowed again, she was just the woman
to give it to him.

She made a great show of tucking her legs under her,
deliberately positioning herself so that her knee pressed
into his thigh. From beneath her eyelashes she watched
to see the effect she was having on him. He looked like
a bronze sculpture—all muscle and power. But she'd be

willing to bet that she'd shot his blood pressure up a notch or two.

Next she propped her arm along the back of the swing, letting her fingers make casual contact with the back of his neck. There was no mistaking the goose bumps there. Excellent.

Then she dipped her head in a way that made the fat shiny braid of golden hair slide over her shoulder and rest provocatively on her right breast. The smile she gave him was designed to melt every wax candle in Tupelo right down to its wick.

"I'll tell you a little secret, Samuel. A woman like me never has to worry about money." She winked.

His eyebrow lifted sardonically and his jaw pulsed with the jumping of tightened muscles.

"That's what I suspected."

"Oh, and you were right." She leaned so close to him that the end of her braid brushed his arm. "I never intended to be one of the huge colony of starving artists in Paris. You'd be surprised at the ways a clever girl like me can make money."

"Nothing you do would surprise me."

She winked again. "Good. I'm glad you understand." She reached out to touch his chest. "And Sammy, when we become family, perhaps you can help me."

"Help you?"

"With business matters. You know, contacts and things like that. A man in your position is bound to know lots of people." She rubbed his cheek. "I think family should help each other, don't you?"

He was on the verge of apoplexy when he heard her chuckle. At first it was a small sound, stifled behind her free hand, and then it was a full-bodied roar of mirth.

He'd been had. She'd used innuendo so cleverly that he'd been completely taken in. He had to admire her. It wasn't often a person, man or woman, could pull the wool over Samuel Adams's eyes.

The beginnings of a smile made the corners of his mouth quirk upward. "Congratulations, Molly. You've accomplished what few men ever do."

His smile widened, and she saw the laugh lines around his eyes. She'd never have guessed that Samuel Adams smiled with his eyes.

Still smiling, he added, "For a moment there, you got the best of me."

She relaxed but she didn't retreat. She kept her hand on his neck and her knee pressed against his thigh. There was no telling when she'd need to use sneaky tactics again. "I can assure you, Samuel Adams, that we are not after your money."

She wouldn't be the first to come after the Adams fortune, but he saw no reason to tell her that. "I deal with finances every day. I suppose it's only natural that that would be my first thought. I owe you an apology."

"Accepted. But I think you've simply been doing what any good son would do—trying to protect your mother."

"You're very generous under the circumstances."

"If it will make you feel better, I'll dump you out of the swing and throw chinaberries at you."

For the first time since they'd met, Samuel laughed. It felt good.

That's how Glory Ethel and Jedidiah found them. As they strolled across the yard, hand in hand, they spotted their children, laughing and swinging under the chinaberry tree.

"Just listen to that, Glory Ethel. The sweet music of friendly laughter."

"And would you look at them, Jedidiah? Don't they look sweet sitting on that swing—just like family."

They approached the chinaberry tree unnoticed by Molly and Samuel. Grinning, Jedidiah cleared his throat. The pair on the swing jumped apart.

"My goodness..." Molly's hand flew to her throat.

"We didn't see you."

Samuel straightened his damp tie and looked guilty, although his mother doubted if he had a darned thing to be guilty about. Didn't she just wish? Lord, it seemed as though she was doomed to a life without grandchildren. But now she had Jedidiah. That was some compensation.

"Well!" She beamed at her son. "It looks like the two of you are getting along just famously."

Samuel exchanged glances with Molly.

"I wouldn't say that." He stood. "Won't you sit down, Mother?"

Molly rose from the swing, her jewelry tinkling as she moved. "Here, Papa. Take my seat."

Glory Ethel and Jedidiah declined.

"We just came out to tell you the good news," Glory Ethel said.

"Good news?"

Molly and Adam spoke simultaneously. He sounded suspicious; she sounded joyful.

"Yes. Jedidiah has invited us to dinner tonight."

Samuel glanced at Molly again. Her eyes were sparkling with pure devilment. No doubt she was planning ahead to the evening, deciding exactly how she would annihilate him. It was a challenge he couldn't resist.

"We accept." He offered his hand to the old man. "Thank you, Mr. Rakestraw."

After they shook hands, Samuel took his mother's elbow and escorted her to the car. Later he'd think of a way to talk his mother out of this foolishness. Right now he had to think of a way to deal with Venus de Molly.

He helped his mother into the car and slid behind the wheel. Back in his own domain, he felt completely in control. He rested his hands on the steering wheel a moment, absorbing the familiar feel of his fine machine. And then he turned the key and the engine purred to life. He drove away from the little house on Robins Street, being careful not to look back.

"He's crazy about me."

His mother's voice startled him. "Who?"

"Jedidiah. Who were you thinking of... As if I had to ask..." She gave him a pleased look.

"Now, Mother. Don't start."

"Who me? I'm just as innocent as a lamb."

"You're as deadly as a lion. Maybe if I told Jedidiah about your true nature, he might change his mind about a wedding."

"Don't you dare."

"You know I would never do anything but sing your praises."

He concentrated on driving, but in the back of his mind he was thinking of a woman in a pair of gold snake sandals and five pounds of turquoise jewelry. Taming her just might prove to be entertaining.

Jedidiah stood in his front yard and watched until the Rolls-Royce was out of sight.

"She likes me, Molly."

"Who?"

"Why, Glory Ethel, that's who. Where in the world is your mind?"

"About two blocks away in a Rolls-Royce Silver Cloud."

"That's what I thought. He's a fine-looking man, isn't he?"

"He's a pain in the . . ."

"Association with artists has added a new dimension to your character, my dear." Laughing, he kissed her on the cheek.

"I love you, Papa."

"I've always known that."

"Yes. But I want you to hear it, as well." She put her arms around him and laid her head on his shoulder. "Papa, I'm going to do everything in my power to see that you're happy."

Straightening, she stared over his head at the chinaberry tree. Its branches were swaying gently in the breeze, whispering the secrets of her childhood. After her mother had died, struck down by cancer at the age of twenty-eight, Molly had retreated to the shelter of another chinaberry tree—one on Papa's farm. In the swaying of the leaves and the sighing of the gentle breezes, she had heard the voices. Perhaps at that moment of her greatest need, the tree itself had come alive to comfort her. Or maybe God had given her heightened perception to help her get through the bad times. Whatever the magic, Molly had never forgotten the lesson. *There are no guarantees, Molly,* the voices had said. *Connections can be broken. Live life to the fullest.*

She had been only eight at the time, but she had never forgotten the lesson.

Each day was a priceless gift, especially to the elderly. If Papa wanted to risk another connection, if he wanted Glory Ethel, she'd see that he got her, and nothing would stand in the way. Certainly not Samuel Adams.

Molly helped Jedidiah get the house ready for the dinner party. They had both decided a candle-lit dinner at home would be cozier than going to a restaurant. Besides, it would allow them more privacy, more time to get to know one another.

Molly picked fresh flowers from the yard—fragrant gardenias from the large bush on the north side of the house, roses from the rampant vines that climbed the backyard fence, and Queen Anne's lace that formed a border between Papa and his next-door neighbor. With an artist's eye, she arranged the flowers and scattered them throughout the house so that they looked as if they might have sprung up on their own in the nooks and crannies of the 1930s house.

"That looks lovely, Molly." Jedidiah took his daughter's hand and spun her around. "And so do you. Like a moonbeam."

Molly laughed and straightened his tie. "We want to impress this woman, don't we?"

"Absolutely." He was thoughtful for a moment, gazing into space, looking back in time. "You know, Molly, when I first started this correspondence I didn't have any plans for romance. I was just lonely."

"I know, Papa. And I'm sorry."

"It's not your fault, baby. You have your career, and I'm proud of that. That's the way it should be." He brushed a piece of lint off his sleeve. "When I got that first letter from Glory Ethel, I knew she was a special woman, someone I could enjoy. We've been writing for a little over a year now, and I feel as if I've known her all my life." He gave his daughter a serious look. "I really think the time is right for both of us, Molly."

"You have my full support, Papa."

"Good. Then you won't mind doing a little thing for me, will you?"

His devilish grin made her suspicious. "Papa...what are you up to?"

"Nothing. I just thought a little entertainment might be nice."

"I agree. Does she like Glenn Miller records?"

"I was thinking of live entertainment."

"Now, Papa..."

"I want Glory Ethel to see what a talented daughter I have. And besides that, she'll be tickled to death with it."

Molly hesitated only a moment, but there was never any doubt in her mind that she would give in to Papa's request. She could never deny her father anything.

Suddenly she grinned. "Well, why not? I might just unbend a steel-plated tyrant."

She hurried to her room to make sure she had everything she needed for the entertainment.

"How do I look?"

Glory Ethel stood nervously on the front porch of Jedidiah's house, patting imaginary wrinkles in her dress.

"You look gorgeous, Mother." Samuel smiled gently at her.

She patted his cheek. "So do you. Every woman should have a son so handsome." She straightened ~er shoulders. "You can ring the bell now."

He did.

Molly answered the door. It was the fi~ woman had ever left Samuel Adams breath~

only vaguely aware of his mother saying something about Jedidiah and disappearing down the hall, for Molly had his full attention. She was wearing a diaphanous dress that looked as if it had floated down from the sky and wrapped itself around her. The dress was as light and airy as moonbeams, and it clung to her curves and nestled in her hollows like a jealous lover. At first he thought the dress was blue, and then he thought it was silver. Finally he decided it was magic.

My God, not only was the woman a hellion, she was also a sorceress. Fortunately, he knew exactly how to deal with *them*.

Bending gallantly at the waist, he took her hand between both of his. "My dear, it's been entirely too long."

Sliding one hand up her arm and turning her palm toward him, he planted a lingering kiss against her skin and had the satisfaction of feeling goose bumps rise on her arm.

His about-face was a surprise to Molly. Fortunately she adored surprises. She threw back her head, and her laughter was as bright as the flashy baubles she wore around her neck.

"Too long for what, Samuel?"

Straightening, he smiled down at her. "Too long to leave a hellion like you alone."

"What's the matter? Afraid I'll think of a diabolical way to pierce that armor you wear?"

He smiled. "No. Too long without a rein."

"A rein?"

"Yes." He reached out and tipped her chin up with one finger. "I discovered long ago that there's only one way to deal with women like you, Molly."

She'd be darned if she'd ask what. Neither would she ˜ʷ any attention to the fresh set of goose bumps he sent skittering over her flesh. She lifted her jaw and glared at him.

"The only way to handle you, my dear, is to tame you."

"Tame me?" She jerked out of his grasp. *"Tame me!"* She stalked down the hallway. When she reached the marble-topped hall table she whirled around and faced him. "I'd just like to see you try!"

He leaned nonchalantly against the doorjamb and smiled at her. But it was not a smile of mirth. It was the cold, deadly smile of a man out to do battle.

"I'd advise you not to issue challenges, my dear. I find them impossible to resist."

"That's not all you're liable to find impossible to resist before this is over." She put her hands on her hips. Her color was high and her eyes sparkled with wrath.

"Anger becomes you, Venus."

She gave him a mock bow. "Thank you, Sir Adams the Bold."

"Don't thank me yet." He moved slowly toward her, pinning her to the spot with his hot, dark eyes. "But you can come closer. I find it impossible to tame a woman who is halfway across the room."

She watched his relentless march across the hall. It put her in mind of Sherman's devastating sweep through the South. She stood her ground. She wasn't Atlanta, and she wasn't about to be burned.

He didn't stop coming until he was so close she could feel his pant leg brushing against her thigh. Maybe she should have worn leather. But who could have predicted this assault?

She steeled herself against his leg pressing through her skirt. "Why don't you come closer? I don't bite."

Her defiance amused him. His eyes danced with mirth as he stared down at her. "Neither do I, my wicked Venus, but I have been known to make even the bold quiver in their boots."

She lifted one long and beautiful leg, just slightly, just enough to cause that moonbeam dress to slither enticingly and bare a portion of calf. "As you can see, I'm not wearing boots."

He stared at that lovely leg just a fraction too long. Her satisfied smile told him so. It wouldn't do to let her get the upper hand, even for a minute.

"I wouldn't advise you to play with fire. You might singe a few hairs on that pretty little head of yours." Taking her arm, he urged her down the hall. "Shall we join our parents?"

"What's the matter, Samuel? Afraid of what I'll do to you out here in the hallway all alone?"

"No. I'm afraid of what *I'll* do to you."

Chapter Three

Molly decided that a graceful retreat would be her best bet at the moment. Anyhow, she'd neglected her hostessing duties too long. She wanted Glory Ethel to love everything about Papa—his house, his dinner, his daughter.

Taking Samuel's hand, she led him into the sitting room. It was a bright and cozy room, filled with chintz and calico, soft watercolors and earthy pottery. There was the fragrance of flowers throughout the room.

Samuel made the space seem smaller. He was a large man, tall and broad shouldered and muscular. But it was more than that, Molly decided. He seemed to dominate the room. He'd chosen a chair that faced the sofa and gave him an unobstructed view of the entire room. Although he appeared to be relaxed and comfortable, she sensed power simmering just beneath the surface. She saw the iron will stamped in every line of his body—from

the carefully controlled expression on his face to the tight
bunching of muscles beneath his dinner jacket.

I wouldn't advise you to play with fire, my dear. The
words he had spoken in the hallway echoed in her mind
as clearly as if he were saying them now. A shiver of excitement went up her spine. She didn't merely love excitement; she thrived on it.

She leaned back in her chair, watching Samuel. He
was discussing organic gardening with Papa as if he'd
invented the method himself. She'd be willing to bet that
he didn't know which end of a spade to put into the
ground. Oh, he was smooth, all right; he was good. And
he had Papa completely fooled. But he didn't fool her.
Not for a minute. He was a deadly cobra waiting to
strike. Molly smiled, thinking ahead to the entertainment she had planned. She was going to give Samuel
Adams something to sink his teeth into when he struck.

"Good girls don't have such wicked smiles."

"What?"

Samuel's voice startled her out of her reverie. He was
leaning close so that his voice was an intimate whisper,
and his hand rested casually on the arm of her chair—so
casually that the touch of his fingers against her arm
appeared to be accidental. Her eyes widened and she
glanced toward the sofa. Papa and Glory Ethel were
deep in conversation. She doubted if they'd notice a herd
of elephants tromping through the room.

"I said—"

"I *know* what you said."

His smile was so devilish she figured he'd had to make
at least one trip to Hades to learn it.

"What's the matter, Molly? Afraid you've gotten
more than you bargained for?"

She assessed him for a full moment before she replied. His black gaze never wavered. She made her smile sweet and her eyes innocent. She knew exactly how to do it. After all, she'd had years of practice at posing.

"Oh, no. I'm merely afraid you aren't up to the challenge."

"You're referring to my old age, I take it."

"No. I'm referring to your inexperience."

One eyebrow lifted and his eyes danced with amusement.

Molly patted his hand in false sympathy. "Samuel, you poor dear. Too busy taking care of all that money at that old bank to have any fun. You're so lucky that I'm going to rescue you."

He threw back his head and roared with laughter. Startled, Glory Ethel and Papa looked up from the sofa.

Glory Ethel glanced from her son to Molly, then back again. "Good grief, Sam, if it's that funny, tell all of us."

"It's just a private joke, Mother."

Jedidiah rose from the sofa and took Glory Ethel's hand. "I'm glad to hear all this laughter in my house. Shall we go in to dinner?" He led Glory Ethel through the door and into the dining room.

Samuel and Molly stood up to follow. He slid one arm around her waist. It was a tiny waist, and it felt altogether too bewitching for his own good; but he was committed to a course of action, and he'd be damned if he'd back down now.

"Shall we follow them, my dear?"

She tilted her head so she could look straight into his eyes. "A private joke, huh?"

"What would you have had me say? That we were playing an elaborate game of seduction?"

"Seduction!"

"That's usually the game men and women play."

The look in his dark eyes did strange things to her heart. She took a moment to catch her breath and recover. Then she gave him a playful pinch on the cheek.

"I'm going to teach you some new games, Samuel."

"I can hardly wait, Venus."

They joined their parents at the dining table, and much to their surprise, the meal was painless. All four of them were sharp-witted people, and the conversation flowed smoothly, covering topics as diverse as flower arranging and stock-market reports.

After the meal was over Molly excused herself, and Jedidiah led his guests into the large and airy music room. Lamplight gleamed across the rich wood of a baby grand piano, and moonlight shone through two enormous arched windows, making a glowing path on the hardwood floor. It was a lovely room, full of charm and graciousness, but what caught Samuel's attention was the enormous watercolor over the mantel. It was a field of flowers, their colors so brilliant they seemed to spill off the canvas and invade the room. Sunlight tipped the edges of the petals and gave the illusion of warming the observer.

He walked closer, lifting his head to gaze up at the work of art.

"Do you like it?" Jedidiah asked.

"It's unbelievable."

"Molly did it. Of all her work, it's my favorite."

Samuel studied the painting. He didn't know much about art, but he had heard that it reflected the spirit and soul of the artist. If that were true, Molly had a soul as rich as the earth and a spirit as freewheeling as the sun. Something in him reached out to the painting, and he felt a tiny glow spring to life in the deep, dark recesses of his own battered and scarred soul.

He continued to gaze at the painting, unable to give up the particular magic that was feeding his spirit. Suddenly there was a sound at the doorway, and he turned.

Molly was standing there, posing. She was both mischievous sprite and lusty *femme fatale*, and she made the room as bright as new copper pennies. She'd been gone only a few minutes, and he was surprised to discover that he had missed her. Not her, he corrected himself. He'd merely missed her particular brand of excitement.

He leaned against the mantel, smiling. He could hardly wait to see what she would do next.

She slowly lowered her hand from the doorframe and began to walk into the room. Her eyes locked on his, and Samuel had no doubt whatsoever that the show was entirely for him.

Molly didn't simply enter a room; she came in like a full-fledged parade. Her feet clicked against the wooden floor and her face was alight with mischief. Samuel peered behind her, expecting to see her followed by a band of pirates, or at the very least a string of prancing ponies.

"I'm sorry I took so long." Her skirts danced around her as she moved.

"That's all right. You are worth waiting for, isn't she?" Jedidiah looked at Samuel for confirmation.

"Indeed, she is." Samuel smiled at Molly to see how she took his hearty declaration. With aplomb. That's how she took it. He would have been disappointed by anything else.

Molly moved toward the piano, gliding across the room directly in the path of moonlight so that she and her dress appeared to be liquid.

"Is everybody ready for the show, Papa?"

Jedidiah beamed and escorted Glory Ethel to the large wing chair beside the piano. Then the spry old man seated himself on the piano bench and ran his fingers lightly over the keys.

Samuel didn't know much about music, but he did know enough to recognize a masterful touch. The old man had talent.

But the person who riveted his attention was Molly. She was leaning against the piano now, her hip pressed against the gleaming wood. Everything except the woman at the piano vanished from Samuel's mind. Moonlight shimmered over her, turning her skin and hair to liquid gold. Lamplight burnished the rich wood so that the piano seemed to flow into and blend with Molly's dress.

Woman and instrument were one. The heavy jazz beat of the music increased, and Molly started singing.

Samuel had never heard anything like it. Her voice was a throaty, bluesy whisper, and she was promising to make a saint turn into a sinner. He didn't doubt it for a minute. He was on the verge of sinning himself.

He called on every resource to combat this strange and disturbing attraction. Reason deserted him. His iron will went into hiding. He told himself it was only a game they were playing. Still, his desire blossomed, rising like a phoenix from the ashes of his harsh and bitter past. He blamed it on the moonlight, he blamed it on the music, he blamed it on fatigue. But even placing blame couldn't make the feelings go away. He wanted to blend with Molly the way the moonlight did. He longed to cover her skin as the moonbeams did—to caress it, to flow over it with his fingers and lips and tongue.

The tempo of the song increased and so did his heart-beat. Molly was promising to be a naughty baby, and he longed for it. His loins were fiery with the need for her to be wicked and wanton and naughtier than all the movie vamps of the twenties.

He leaned heavily against the mantel, more for support than anything else. Molly's voice drugged him. The room seemed to spin away.

He was burning inside—his throat, his chest, his loins, his eyes. She was silk and satin and wind and fire. She was earth and he was rain, pouring through her, washing over her.

And she was music. Jazz flowed around him and through him, and from a distance, Molly's voice drifted to him.

He felt the solid reality of the mantel. Molly was still beside the piano singing and he was still standing in front of the fireplace. To find himself there came as a shock. His fantasy had been so real he could almost taste her lips, could almost feel her flesh pressed against his.

He wiped his hand across the back of his brow and tried to concentrate. There was a musical interlude, and thankfully her sultry voice stopped. But then, to his amazement, she danced across the floor, her shoes marking a sassy rhythm on the polished wood. He suddenly realized that that's why she had disappeared and why she had made such a noise when she had come back: she was wearing tap-dancing shoes.

Jedidiah segued into another song, and Molly stopped dancing and started singing again. This time Samuel recognized the song—"Embraceable You." He'd once dated a woman who had been fond of singing that song—badly, as he remembered. Not like Molly. Not at all like Molly.

The husky voice set him on fire again, but he clung to the mantel and to his sanity—barely. When she sang in that suggestive voice that she wanted her arms about him, he had to clench his hands into fists and ram them into his pockets to keep from obliging.

Finally he became aware that the music had stopped.

Around him there were vague movements and sounds—Jedidiah inviting his mother for a moonlight stroll, and Glory Ethel accepting. But he was lost in song—the remembered melody vibrating through his body and clouding his mind.

Suddenly he felt the swish of gossamer skirts against his knees.

"Papa wanted me to sing."

"I beg your pardon?"

Startled, he looked down into Molly's face. She was standing beside him at the fireplace. His glance swept over the room. It was empty except for the two of them.

"I said, Papa wanted me to sing."

"You do it beautifully."

"Thank you."

His dark eyes seemed lit by the fires of hell and his muscles were bunched tightly under his jacket. Molly felt the tension flowing from him. Her body came alive under his intense scrutiny. She felt both taut and loose at the same time. Part of her was melting and part of her was so tightly wound she wanted to scream. He was a handsome man; virile, desirable. But there was something deadly about him, too.

She backed away from him. He cocked an eyebrow.

"What's the matter, Molly. Afraid?"

"No. Is there any reason I should be?"

He was silent for so long, merely staring at her, that she wet her dry lips with her tongue. Finally he reached out, ever so slowly. She felt the whisper touch against her cheek, the lightest brushing of fingertips against her skin. And then he withdrew the hand.

"I'm a man. And I'm not accustomed to turning down such blatant invitations."

She didn't trust herself to speak.

"The song, Molly. You practically invited me to make love to you. Don't you know how dangerous that is?"

She resisted an urge to put her hand over her racing heart. "It wasn't an invitation."

"What was it, then?"

"Do you really want to know the truth?"

"It would be refreshing to hear the truth."

"Music, dance, drama, painting—Papa loves all the arts." Molly moved toward the wing chair beside the piano as she talked. She felt a restless need to be moving; but more than that, she felt a need to put some distance between herself and Samuel. There was a connection between them; she could feel the tug. And connections were dangerous. She sat in the chair, tucking her feet up and settling her skirt over her legs. "And he made sure that I loved them, too. I was taking voice lessons before I could read. He had visions that I would be one of the great singers—another Billie Holiday or Fanny Brice. The closest I ever came to singing fame was winning the Jersey Queen contest."

"Jersey Queen? As in New Jersey?"

"No. As in cows, Jersey cows." She saw his shoulders shake. "Go ahead. You can laugh. We thought it was pretty darned funny ourselves. But we needed the money, and it was a convenient way to win a scholarship. I was seventeen. We were moving to Chicago and I was headed for college." She paused, searching his face. When she saw nothing except genuine interest, she continued speaking. "I sang and danced to that song. It's been Papa's favorite ever since, and he takes great pride in having me repeat my Miss Jersey performance. I haven't the heart to turn him down."

Samuel was drawn into her story. He pictured Molly at seventeen, singing that torch song. Had she been as beautiful then as she was now? And as deadly?

He drew a ragged breath. In the last few minutes he'd seen exactly how much he was his father's son. It had been a flashy woman who had enticed his father, who had made him give up a wife and two children and the respect of an entire town. Samuel would do whatever it took to keep from being another Taylor Adams.

He hardened his heart and his voice. "Does the song have a name?"

"'Naughty Baby.'"

"It fits."

There it was again, she thought. That remote, cold look that made her want to shake him. "You don't approve of me, do you, Samuel?"

"Quite frankly, no."

"Is it the dress?" She lifted the hem of her skirt and let it float back around her. "The jewelry?" She touched the baubles at her neck. "The tap-dancing shoes?" She stood up and did a quick staccato rhythm on the hardwood floor.

He arched one eyebrow in that sophisticated way he had. Molly felt a surge of anger. This arrogant man, this hell-bent-for-leather *bossy* banker, was ripe for a lesson. And she was going to give it to him. She'd worry about the consequences tomorrow.

Using her best model's gliding walk, she swayed across the room toward him, very much aware of what the moonlight did to her skin and hair and of the enticing way she made her skirt swirl around her legs. She hoped his throat was as dry as ashes from last year's fire.

She didn't stop until she was so close she could see the glowing center of his blacker-than-midnight eyes.

"Or is it this, Samuel?" She looped her arms quickly around his neck and tangled her hands in his hair. Making her voice a seductive purr, she leaned closer. "Am I too much woman for you to handle?"

"You think that, do you?" His voice was low and dangerous, and it sent shivers up her spine.

"Yes." Her smile was inviting and wicked. "You act like a man on the run."

He reacted—not in quick anger, but with slow, sure deliberation. His right hand cupped her cheek, resting there for a small eternity before gliding back into her hair. She felt her scalp tingle as he raked through her heavy tresses and let them drift slowly through his fingers.

He didn't speak. He didn't have to; his eyes said it all. Anger and passion burned there; and something else, something so deep, so mysterious, that Molly felt all the breath leave her body.

With his free hand he pulled her hard against his hips. Her heart climbed high in her chest, and in a quick burst of hindsight she wondered if she had pushed him too far. He tightened his hold and slowly lowered his head.

She felt his warm breath against her cheek, smelled the clean masculine scent of him, heard his deep intake of air. And then his lips were on hers. There was no tenderness in the kiss, no genuine feeling, no warmth, no great desire. It was the kiss of an experienced man, an expert; a knowing kiss performed with all the artfulness of a master deceiver.

In spite of that, she let herself go, straining close and enjoying the kiss with every vibrant fiber in her body.

Samuel's lips moved over hers, coaxing, demanding, sensual, and he felt the full voltage of her response. Danger signals clanged in his head. Pulling back, he gazed down at her. She was flushed and lovely, and he discovered that he was more vulnerable than he had thought.

It was an entire minute before he could speak.

"I never let a challenge go unanswered."

She pressed two fingers to her lips and felt their slight tremble. She was amazed at this man's power over her, but she pressed on. Cowardice was not her style.

"Neither do I, Samuel." She backed away and leaned against the mantel. "Just remember this: you were the one who kissed me."

"I wasn't kissing you, Molly. I was taming you. There's a difference."

"I suppose a man of your vast experience has a little black book of excuses that cover a multitude of sins."

"A man of my experience knows how to give a woman what she wants. But beware who you entice, Molly. Not all men will kiss and retreat. If you behave that way, you're asking for trouble."

"I wasn't enticing you. I was merely teaching you a lesson."

"You've missed your calling. You make a delightful teacher."

"You're laughing, and this is no laughing matter."

"You're absolutely right." He ran his hand over his face as if he were wiping away his grin. "Tell me, Molly, what was that lesson you taught me?"

"I was trying to teach you that you'll always find the things you expect. Look for the worst, and that's what you'll get."

"You don't have to rationalize your behavior for me, my dear. You've wanted to be kissed from the minute I walked through your door tonight. And I obliged."

Color blazed in her cheeks. "I have not!"

"That dress, those teasing, flirty looks, that provocative song. I'm thirty-five years old. There isn't much I haven't seen or done."

"If you're trying to tell me you're jaded, don't bother. Your kiss already said that."

He took her swiftly this time—without fanfare, without warning and without mercy. His mouth was hard and punishing.

The air left her lungs and the starch left her knees. She clung to his shoulders for support. A part of her battled against him, resisted him, and another part surrendered. It was a dangerous game she was playing, and she knew it. But, ahh, it was exciting. And Molly loved excitement.

Moaning, she opened her mouth for the invasion of his tongue. She felt its rough abrasion as he plunged briefly inside; and then abruptly he withdrew.

Releasing her, he stepped back as casually as if he'd just returned from the corner convenience store with a loaf of bread.

"You like to play games, don't you, Molly?"

"Yes." She longed to press her hands to her hot cheeks, but she wouldn't give him that satisfaction.

He put his hand into his coat pocket for his pipe, and then he remembered that he'd given up smoking last year when his blood pressure had started creeping up. He'd have to face Molly without a crutch.

"Then be warned, my dear. I don't play anybody's game. I live by my own rules."

"There's something you should know about *me*, Samuel. I believe rules were made to be broken."

His eyes darkened. "I loved a person like that once."

His voice was so filled with passion and pain that Molly spoke in a whisper. "Who?"

"My father."

The room because hushed and still. Molly stared at the raw pain in Samuel's face and felt a great remorse. She'd always lived for the moment, lived for fun and excitement and joy. But never had she inflicted hurt. She had a marshmallow heart that caused her to cry over every unfortunate creature—stray cats without homes, fallen birds with broken wings, abused dogs with cruel masters.

Impulsively she reached toward his face.

Samuel turned abruptly and walked away from her. Sitting down in the wing chair beside the piano, he smiled. "It seems that we are left with time on our hands, my dear. Sing for me."

Molly looked at that sad, brittle smile, and great tears welled up in her heart. But she didn't cry. Samuel would have hated it. His proud bearing told her how much he would have despised any sympathy.

Assuming a nonchalant manner, she walked over to the piano. "I can't play as well as Papa, but here goes."

The sound of music filled the room, and then she began to sing "Someone to Watch Over Me."

Chapter Four

By the time Samuel and his mother left the Rake-straws, it was well after midnight. They didn't talk on the drive back to their hotel. Glory Ethel leaned her head against the seat and relived her walk with Jedidiah, and afterward, their cozy visit, sitting in his comfortable den, talking and listening to records.

Samuel tried desperately to rationalize his encounter with Molly. But no matter how he twisted and turned things in his mind, it didn't change the fact. He had kissed Molly; and he had enjoyed it.

That bit of self-knowledge so disturbed him that he didn't even chide Glory Ethel for staying out late with Jedidiah. They were both silent, lost in their own thoughts, as they rode the elevator up to the third floor.

"Night, Sammy."

"Good night, Mother."

Samuel undressed methodically, as he always did. First he loosened his tie. Then he sat in a chair and removed his shoes and socks. Next he removed his jacket, then his tie, then his shirt, taking time to hang each item carefully in the closet. He finished his ritual by taking off his pants and his shorts.

He climbed into bed and waited for the soothing coolness of the sheets to work their usual magic. He was an organized, methodical man with a routine and a schedule for everything, including falling asleep. It took five minutes usually; ten if he'd had an especially worrisome day.

Twelve-thirty came, and twelve-forty, and twelve forty-five. At one o'clock he looked once more at the watch he'd carefully placed on the bedside table. The luminous dial mocked him.

"Dammit." He put the watch back on the table and pulled the sheet over his head. He closed his eyes and willed his mind to become a blank.

Music drifted through his consciousness. In a drowsy half-haze he saw her: the shiny blond hair, the bangles, the gaudy costume. She was singing "Help Me Make It Through The Night." A tall man was walking toward her, a distinguished man with gray at his temples: Taylor, his father. The floozy lowered the mike and he saw her face clearly. It was Betsy, the homebreaker. The man took her in his arms and started kissing her. Betsy wrapped her arms around him, dragging him to the floor.

They were in each other's arms. Samuel moaned in his sleep. And suddenly the man wasn't Taylor; it was Samuel, and he could feel the press of the woman's sweet, hot flesh. She twisted beneath him, seeking him with her red lips. He lifted himself on his elbow and looked into her face. But it wasn't Betsy he saw; it was Molly—Molly with her creamy skin and her hypnotic turquoise eyes, Molly with a body so perfect it was sculpted in bronze.

Samuel grew crazy with need. He ripped her gaudy clothes aside. She was soft and lush. She was full of mystery and wonder. And she beckoned to him. He entered that softness, was consumed by it.

He took her and she was his. Together they soared. A cry burst from his lips, a joyful cry of completion. Molly lay under him, her soft curves fitted intimately against his body.

Suddenly he felt a chill. Molly's warm skin became cold and hard. He lifted himself on his elbow and looked down at her. She was a statue, a perfect body captured forever in bronze for the whole world to see.

She wasn't his at all. She belonged to every man.

Samuel awakened, sweating. He kicked the covers aside and sat up in bed, one hand groping for his watch. Nine o'clock. He'd never slept that late in his life.

He ran his hand through his hair and started toward the shower when he saw the note under his door.

Sammy, it read. *Jedidiah is showing me the city. Don't expect me back until late. Mother.*

"Damn."

He wadded the note into a ball and threw it into the garbage can. It bounced off the rim and rolled onto the floor. He said another word, and bent over to pick it up.

His knees popped. He was getting old. He *felt* old.

He climbed into the shower and told himself he'd take the day to do business. He had a briefcase full of reports that demanded his attention. No sooner had he soaped his chest than he realized he wasn't going to do business at all that day. He was going to visit Molly.

He closed his eyes and let the water cascade over his chest. He remembered her skin, the way it had looked in the moonlight. His eyes snapped open. This meeting would be strictly business. He would try to talk sensibly to her about stopping this foolishness between his mother and Jedidiah.

He would put an end to this madness and get out of Tupelo before it was too late.

Too late for what? his inner voice mocked him.

He stepped out of the shower and dried himself so vigorously, the towel burned his skin. The only person in danger here was his mother. He was going to visit Molly strictly to protect his mother.

Molly always had three or four projects going at the same time. With Papa gone for the day, today was perfect for repotting the houseplants, cleaning the hall closet, updating a couple of her cocktail dresses and catching up on her correspondence.

When the doorbell rang she had her hands in a clay pot full of philodendrons and potting soil.

"Coming." She left the pot on the kitchen table with the feathers and beads she was putting on a red satin dress and the unfinished letters she was writing, and made her way to the front door.

"My goodness." She put her hand on her cheek and left a smudge of dirt.

Samuel was standing there, dressed in a suit and tie and white shirt, as immaculate as always, but looking somehow vulnerable and uncertain.

"I don't usually drop by uninvited..." He stopped speaking, caught up by Molly's turquoise eyes. Willing himself to break the spell, he started over: "I *never* drop by uninvited, but..." Words failed him again as he stared down at Molly. He'd never known how becoming dirt could seem when teamed with turquoise eyes.

She smiled. "I *love* unexpected company." Taking his hand, she pulled him through the door. "Do come in."

He didn't even notice that she got dirt on his hand.

She led him through the hall, following a trail of potting soil to the kitchen.

"I woke up this morning and thought, with Papa gone, what a perfect day for projects. Don't you think Tuesday is a perfect day for projects?"

"Wednesday."

"What?"

"Today is Wednesday."

"My goodness! I thought the morning paper had put the date down wrong. And calendars are always so confusing. You can't even tell what's going on unless you already know the date, and why bother to look if you already know?"

In all his life he'd never met anybody who lived without benefit of a calendar, a schedule. He felt as if he had been dunked in a pool of refreshing lemonade. He laughed, and the sound of his mirth echoed around the sunny kitchen.

"I've never known the date on a newspaper to be wrong, Molly. You might use it to keep track of the days."

"If I ever run out of exciting things to do and have to keep track of the days, I will."

"How do you keep your appointments?"

"Robin."

"A secretary? A girlfriend? A bird?" To his amazement, Samuel was feeling positively frivolous.

"No. A male friend. We share an apartment."

Samuel felt a punch in his gut that was nothing short of pure, primitive jealousy.

"I see."

Molly saw the sudden stiffness of his back, the tightness of his face.

Yesterday afternoon she would have taken issue, would have done battle. But not now, not after what Samuel had said last night: *I loved a person like that once.... My father.*

Her heart swelled with sympathy and she put a hand on his arm. "It's not like that at all."

"You don't owe me any explanations."

"I know. But I don't want any misunderstandings ... because of Papa and your mother." She released his arm and walked to the cabinet. A quick swipe with the tea towel removed most of the dirt from her hands, but did nothing for her face. Samuel, watching her intently, was glad. He was bewitched by that one small spot on her cheek.

Taking down two cups, she poured coffee, shoved aside the feathers and placed the coffee on the table. "Robin is a dedicated artist, a good man, a dear friend, and not at all interested in me." Molly indicated the cups. "Coffee?"

"Thanks."

"Cream? Sugar?"

"Black."

Samuel sat down at the table beside Molly and took a fortifying sip of black coffee. It didn't make him feel a damned bit better. The man—Robin—was obviously a fool.

He looked at Molly over the rim of his cup. His fingers itched to wipe away that beguiling smudge of potting soil on her cheek. Things were getting out of hand. He decided to change the subject, to talk business, but he couldn't even remember what business he'd come to talk about. A vision of Molly and Robin clouded his mind.

"Do you pose for him?"

"Yes."

"I see."

"It's strictly professional."

"I have a hard time seeing how any man can be impersonal about your body."

"You're not an artist."

"No. I'm merely a banker."

The look on Samuel's face reminded her of Mickey after he'd jumped on the sofa and knocked over a vase of flowers. She'd always been a soft touch for that look. Reaching across the table, Molly covered his hand with hers. "Samuel, let's not fight today."

His smile was bittersweet. "Were we fighting?"

"Not quite, but almost. When I really fight, I throw things." She took a sip of coffee, then grinned impishly at him over the rim of the cup. "Cheap things, though. I'm no fool."

He chuckled, and suddenly he realized how easy it was to laugh with Molly. Leaning back in his chair, he relaxed a little. "Agreed, then. We won't fight. I'll be going soon, anyhow. Surely we can maintain a truce for the next fifteen minutes."

"You're leaving?"

"I have a briefcase full of work at the hotel."

With a burst of insight, Molly realized she didn't want him to go. She didn't know why, nor did she stop to question it. She merely acted on instinct.

"Before you go would you mind doing something for me?"

"Anything that doesn't involve your lethal water hose."

"I promise; this won't get you wet." Feeling happy and mischievous, she set her coffee cup down and picked up the red satin dress. "Would you mind putting this on?"

"That's not my quite my style."

"You needn't look so horrified. I don't have kinky games in mind. I just need a dummy."

"The last time anybody checked me out, I didn't qualify."

"A dressmaker's dummy." Laughing, she stood, holding the red dress out for his inspection. "See. I've ripped out the side seams so you won't have any trouble at all getting into it."

He eyed the dress suspiciously. "And then what?"

"And then I can tell exactly where to put all this." She picked up a handful of beads and feathers from the table.

Samuel had never done anything remotely connected to sewing before. And he would have been horrified if anybody had suggested he take part in a dressmaking scheme. But Molly was standing there with dirt on her face, looking expectantly at him with those big turquoise eyes, and he knew there was no way he would turn her down. At the moment, if she had asked him to stand on his head and recite the Gettysburg Address backward, he would have tried.

He shoved his coffee cup aside. "If word of this gets back to Florence, my reputation is ruined."

"Does that mean you'll do it?"

"Against my better judgment. Exactly what is it I'm supposed to do?"

"All you have to do is stand still."

It sounded simple enough. Samuel pushed back his chair and stood.

Molly sized him up. "I never realized how tall you are."

He smiled at her. "Should I apologize?"

"No. Just bend over."

He ducked his head and she moved in close with the red satin dress. She smelled of rich loamy earth and fresh summer flowers and something else—something so intoxicating he had to fight to keep his desire under control.

She slipped the dress over his head.

"What is that scent you're wearing?" His voice was muffled by the red satin.

"What?"

She lifted the folds of the dress and stuck her head under the skirt. They stood face-to-face under the cover of red satin. His head was slightly inclined and hers was tilted upward.

Samuel sucked in his breath and Molly wet her lips with the tip of her tongue. He cleared his throat, and she blushed. They stared at each other, as aware as two wild deer preparing to mate.

Her voice dropped to a whisper. "I didn't hear what you said."

"I said..." Her eyes were so intensely blue they made him forget.

"Yes?"

Her breathless voice started his heart racing.

"That fragrance... what is it?"

"It's called Night of a Thousand Splendors."

Night of a Thousand Splendors. At the moment, he could envision at least nine hundred ninety-nine of them. And all with Molly. Her heady fragrance washed over him and he leaned close—so close he could feel her warm breath upon his throat.

"Molly..."

She braced one hand against his chest and tipped her head farther back. Underneath her palm she felt the strong pulsing of his heart, the solid strength of his muscles.

"Yes, Samuel?"

His head tipped close. He was so close now, he could almost taste her lips. It was his dream that saved him. Suddenly he saw himself, as besotted and foolhardy as his father, completely taken in by a beautiful, flamboyant woman.

He straightened. "Don't you think this dress is a little small for the two of us?"

Her laugh was shaky. "My goodness. How like me to get sidetracked."

Hastily she ducked down and out of the dress and pulled it completely over his head. Her eyes were bright and her cheeks were flushed. She tugged and pulled on the dress, adjusting it to his big body, talking nervously as she worked.

"I guess you'll find that out about me, Samuel. I distract easily. Just one little word sets me off on a tangent. I completely forget what I was doing in the first place." As she smoothed the dress over his chest, she felt the tensing of his muscles. A tremor started somewhere deep inside her and she had to struggle to keep it out of her voice. "The day you came—my goodness, was it only yesterday?—I was digging up the flower bed and suddenly I wound up in a water fight with the dogs. And then *you* came along..."

"Molly." He grasped her shoulders gently, interrupting her flow of words.

"What?"

He smiled down at her. Betsy, his father's lover, had been beautiful—probably still was, for all he knew—but she had never been enchantingly innocent. In spite of what Molly did—posing nude and having her body sculpted and painted for all the world to see—she looked as innocent and fresh and appealing as an untouched rosebud.

He reached up and tenderly touched her cheek. "You have dirt on your face." Gazing deeply into her eyes, he wiped away the smudge.

Molly was accustomed to the companionship of men. In Paris she'd had a least a dozen suitors—all handsome men who loved to dance and laugh and play lively games. But none of them were like Samuel. Not one had had that haunted look in the eyes, as if all the demons in hell were in pursuit and only she could save him. And not one of them had had that exquisitely tender touch.

She closed her eyes and let the feel of his hands wash over her.

Samuel's hand lingered on her face. Her skin was dangerously soft. He found himself wanting to burrow close to her fragrant skin, to press his lips and his nose to the spot his fingers touched, to capture the essence of her with all his senses.

No woman had ever made him feel that way—sentimental and passionate at the same time. He'd made damned sure of that. Or had he? Had he really kept women at a proper distance in his life, or was it all fate? His mother, a woman of foolish romantic notions, had always told him that fate was just waiting for the right moment to send that one special woman his way. He'd thought it was hogwash and had told her so.

Molly made him wonder.

He circled his thumb against her beguiling cheek one last time.

"There. That should do it." His hand abandoned her cheek.

"Thank you." She reached up and put two fingers on the spot he had touched.

"Anytime."

"You wouldn't say that if you knew how often I dig in the dirt—and how often it ends up on my face instead of in the flowerpots where it belongs."

He gave her a long, penetrating look that took her breath away. "Perhaps I would, Molly."

Looking at him, she felt as if she had reached up and touched the sun. It took her a full two minutes to cast off the spell.

Finally she backed away from Samuel and picked up a pincushion and a handful of brightly colored feathers.

"Time to get to work. Now you just hold still."

"That's what you said the last time . . . before we got sidetracked."

"No sidetracking this time. It will all be strictly business. I promise."

She reached up to pin a feather on the neckline of the dress, and her hand brushed against his chin. Sudden awareness of him sizzled through her again, and the motion of her hands ceased.

He put one hand over hers. "Do you break promises as easily as you break rules, Molly?"

She lifted her gaze to him. "No. I never break a promise."

"Never?"

"Never."

He pressed his index finger on her throat over her wildly fluttering pulse. The finger drew a circle on her skin and then moved slowly upward, sending heat waves through her body.

She couldn't move, she couldn't breathe. She stood still, staring at him with big, wondering eyes and feeling the heat of his touch consume her.

"I could take that as a challenge, Molly."

His finger found her lips and traced their sensuous outline. She waited, unable to move, unwilling to break the spell that bound them. Slowly, ever so slowly, he parted her lips and slipped his finger inside.

"Hmm." The moan slipped out, a deep groan of satisfaction that Molly couldn't control, didn't want to control. She closed her mouth around his finger and dragged her tongue across his skin.

"My God, Molly."

Samuel pulled her into his arms, heedless of feathers and beads and propriety. The pincushion dropped from her nerveless fingers, and pins and feathers went flying all over the kitchen floor.

Samuel's mouth came down on hers. He'd meant to tame her, to prove to himself that he was a man completely in charge but the minute his lips touched hers he was lost. *She* tamed *him*, controlled him, conquered him. And still he felt the victor.

As he savored the sweet nectar of her kiss, he felt a rapture sweep through his soul. He felt an uplifting, affirmative joy that he had thought reserved for books and movies with fairy-tale endings. In a fog of wonder, he clung to her, cleaved to her and kissed her with the tender passion of a man obsessed.

Neither of them heard the doggie door bang open. Mickey and Minnie pranced into the kitchen for their

usual midmorning snack. What they found instead were
the feathers. With joyful barks they attacked the bright
playthings on the floor, catching the feathers in their
mouths and chasing each other under the kitchen table
and around the kitchen chairs.

They ran between Samuel's legs twice before he even
noticed them.

Finally Mickey, blinded by the mouthful of feathers
that floated up into his eyes, banged heavily against the
backs of Samuel's knees. He became aware that he'd
been kissing Molly for some time now, and probably
would have gone on kissing her forever.

Easing his hold, he clung for one last sweet moment
to her lips, and then he broke away. She looked flushed
and lovely and so desirable, she made his heart ache.

He was clearly in danger. In an effort to save himself,
he resorted to teasing.

"If I'd known dressmaking was like this, I might have
taken it up years ago."

Molly unconsciously pressed her hands against her
lips, as if to save his kiss. Mickey barked, and Minnie
nipped at her heels. For the first time ever, she wanted
to swat them.

"What have you done?" She addressed her dogs, but
her question was as much for Samuel as for her pets.
What he had done was press all the right buttons so that
she was in his arms, a willing captive, a woman who
forgot the lessons of the past and jeopardized the freewheeling future merely for a moment's heady pleasure.
She lived for the moment and she lived for excitement,
but she lived without connections—except for Papa. She
didn't want connections. They hurt. How could she have
forgotten that?

Hastily she bent over the dogs and began to pluck feathers out of their mouths. "How can I create a ravishing frock if you two eat the feathers?"

A yellow feather dropped out of Mickey's mouth and floated to the floor. Suddenly Molly saw a vision of her mother, her face smiling and her hair so bright it rivaled the sun. If it hadn't been for Samuel's kiss and his tender caresses, the feather might have been nothing more than a feather. But now it was symbolic of the mother she had loved and lost.

A tear slipped from under her lashes and trickled down her cheeks. She hated being weak and vulnerable, even for a moment, and she sought to hide it by softly chiding her dogs again. "What have you done?"

Samuel was astonished. He had been smiling down at Molly, both amused and touched by the sight of the lively woman and her frolicking pets. And now there was a bright tear on her cheek.

He squatted quickly beside her. "Hey, now, there's no need to cry. I'll help you clean up the mess."

"It's not the dogs." Her lips trembled, and another tear slipped out.

"Molly?" Samuel cupped her face and gently tilted it so that she was staring directly into her eyes. The glitter of tears affected him in an astonishing way. He wanted to pick up a sword and do battle, to annihilate everything that was remotely connected with Molly's tears. His thumbs rubbed her chin. "What, then? Tell me."

"Promise you won't laugh?"

"I promise." He comforted her with gentle strokes on her cheeks. "I could never laugh at a woman's tears, especially a woman with such compelling eyes." He saw the glimmer of a smile on her face. "Please tell me."

"Sometimes I'm silly.... I see one thing and it reminds me of another...." She paused to take a steadying breath and to give him another shaky smile. "And before you know it, I'm crying."

"Is that all?"

"Yes."

"I think there's more."

"You promised you wouldn't laugh, and you didn't. Thank you."

"You're very welcome." Still he squatted, and still he caressed her cheek. "Tell me why you were crying this time, Molly."

Papa was the only person she'd ever confided in. She supposed that her naturally sunny disposition made the need for a confidant unimportant. Whatever her reasons, she now found herself in the unique position of confiding in a man, a man unrelated to her in any way except... Her mind groped for the right words. Was it a connection of the heart?

She lifted her tear-streaked face and studied Samuel. The connection was there. She felt it. Prickles raked her skin and a cold wind blew over her soul. Since her mother's death, she'd never allowed herself to form a close relationship. Papa was the exception, of course. He was always there, as reliable as the sun and as unchangeable as the land.

Samuel was still waiting for her explanation.

She'd always hated lying, but on the other hand, she felt the danger of telling him her true feelings. It was almost like inviting him into her heart.

She decided to tell Samuel quickly and get it over with. Then she would definitely, absolutely, get this relationship back on a casual basis.

"It was the yellow feathers, Samuel. They reminded me of my mother's hair, and then I started thinking about her death, and before you know it, I was crying."

"I'm so sorry." His voice was tender.

"Thank you."

"You're a complicated woman, Molly Rake-straw..." His hands lingered on her face. "And a dangerous one, too."

"Dangerous?"

He wasn't ready to give an honest answer to that probing question. Instead he took her hands and lifted her to her feet.

"With the pins. I'm not so sure I can trust you not to attach a few feathers to my chest."

While he spoke, he examined her face. She seemed to buy his explanation. That was a relief. The situation was close to being out of control. And he could *never* relinquish control.

"I promise I won't attach feathers to your chest..." She paused to give him an impish grin. "...Unless I decide you look good in yellow feathers."

"I take back everything I said. You're not merely dangerous—you're formidable, too."

She wielded the pincushion like a sword. "That's because I have the pins."

Their laughter lightened the mood. For the next twenty minutes Molly arranged beads and feathers over his chest, cocking her head this way and that, studying her handiwork as if she were creating a Dior original. From time to time she had him parade across the kitchen floor so she could get the full effect.

He obliged. Not only did he do her bidding, but he went even further and added a few steps of his own.

Molly laughed so hard, tears came into her eyes. But this time, they were tears of happiness.

Samuel thought that he'd always like to see her that way—her head tilted back, her bright hair swinging and her face alight with joy.

They took a late lunch break, and then Molly enlisted his help in repotting her plants.

"I know less about horticulture than I do about dresses," he told her.

"This doesn't require knowledge—merely a willingness to get your hands dirty."

"I guess there has to be a first time."

"You never played in the dirt?"

"I don't think my board members would approve."

She started to make a retort about his childhood, and then she saw his expression. It was as earnest and serious as if he were facing a bank board. A part of her cried for all the small joys he must have missed, and with that, a little piece of her heart became forever his.

She put a happy lilt in her voice. "They're not here today and I'll never tell."

"Then lead me to the dirt."

She happily dragged three philodendrons off the front porch and declared them puny. For the first time since his childhood, Samuel got his hands in the dirt. And it felt good.

He patted soil around a newly potted plant and smiled at Molly. "A man could get addicted to this."

"I've always found digging in the earth to be therapeutic." She wiped a stray tendril off her face and got another smudge of dirt on her cheek.

He studied the beguiling smudge. It wasn't repotting plants that was addictive; it was the woman. All his senses went on alert. He'd come to her house this morning for a simple business talk, and he'd stayed all day. What kind of madness was that?

"It must be getting very late." That was as good an excuse as any for leaving. He glanced at his watch to emphasize the statement.

"I don't know. I try not to think about time."

A woman like Molly could drive a man crazy. He took his hands out of the flowerpot and glanced at her— quickly, so that his gaze wouldn't linger on the smudge.

"I *always* think about time. And it's time for me to go." He set the newly potted plant in the center of the table, then started to the door. "Goodbye, Molly. Thanks for lunch."

Molly looked at his determined back, his long strides. He would soon be out the door.

"Don't go. Not yet."

He turned at the sound of her soft entreaty. Molly was standing beside the kitchen table with one outstretched hand. He had a vision of her with her face uptilted and lips softly parted. In his mind he saw her with tears on her cheeks.

He took a quick step toward her. "Molly?"

The connection pulled at her, making her yearn forward. She saw a light come on in his dark eyes. It was more than she could handle.

She stepped back and leaned against the kitchen table. "You forgot to wash your hands."

The flames in his eyes went out.

"So I did."

He washed them quickly and left before he could change his mind.

Chapter Five

Samuel opened his hotel door on the first knock. Glory Ethel was standing in the hallway.

"Mother, where on earth have you been?"

"Didn't you get my note?" She came into his room, closing the door behind her.

"Yes. But you forgot to mention that you'd be out long enough to give me ulcers." Samuel wasn't in the best of moods. He stalked to a chair beside the window and picked up the report he'd been trying to read for the last two hours. Snapping the papers, he scowled at his mother.

"I know you don't approve, but I didn't think you'd be so fierce." Laughing, she put her hands over her breasts. "Spare me son, for I've done no wrong."

"That's not funny, Mother. I happen to be working on a complicated business matter." He held the report in a death grip, frowning over the top of the page.

Glory Ethel sat down in the chair opposite her son and studied him closely. She didn't miss a thing.

"Is that dirt under your fingernails, Sammy?"

"Yes. I got it helping Molly repot plants."

"You repotted plants?"

He looked up and scowled. "Is that a crime?"

Glory Ethel thought it was wonderful, but she knew better than to tell him so. "No, it's no crime." She settled back in her chair. Her own news could wait. "So, you visited Molly today?"

"Yes."

Extracting information from him was going to be worse than pulling wisdom teeth, but she was determined. "What did you do besides repot plants?"

He looked her straight in the eye. "If you want to know whether we became good friends and whether today changed my mind about you marrying Jedidiah, the answer is no." He looked down at his reports, and the sight of the dirt reminded him of the smudge on Molly's cheek. He was totally unaware of the way his expression softened. "Besides, we didn't have time to discuss the wedding. I was too busy helping Molly with her sewing."

"You helped with *sewing*?"

He jerked his head up, aware that he'd told her something he'd fully meant to keep a secret. "Mother, what is it with you? You've repeated everything I've said. Are you getting hard of hearing?"

Glory Ethel wanted to jump up and shout hallelujah for the things her son had told her; she wanted to sing the praises of the lively young woman who had loosened up her son, if only for a day, but she was far too wise. She crossed her hands in her lap and looked serene.

"I suppose I'm a little addled by my own news.... Jedidiah and I have set a wedding date."

The future Sam had planned so carefully—for all of them—shattered right before his eyes. It was too late to stop the wedding now, and besides that, his mother *did* look happy.

"I'm sorry I'm so grouchy. Too much on my mind, I guess." He got up from his chair and hugged her. "Congratulations, Mother. All I want is for you to be happy." He returned to his chair and gave her his full attention. "Now, tell me your plans."

On the other side of town in the little house on Robins Street, Molly was hearing the same news from her father.

"The wedding will be in Tupelo, Molly, but Glory Ethel wants to give a big engagement party in Florence next week. She's anxious for us to meet all her friends. She and Samuel are leaving today to start preparations."

Molly loved parties. She adored meeting new people. She was thrilled for Papa and had told him so. But she felt a strange reluctance to go to Florence.

"Are you sure I need to be there, Papa? Since I spend most of my time in Paris and will rarely see her friends, I see no real reason for me to go."

"Are you feeling all right, Molly?" Jedidiah scooted over on the sofa where the two of them were sitting and put his hand on his daughter's forehead. "I've never known you to turn down a party invitation, and you've been unusually subdued this evening."

"I'm fine, Papa." Feeling a little contrite, she took his hand. "And I'm *very* happy for you and Glory Ethel."

"You don't look happy. If you're worried about me, honey, there's no need. I loved your mother more than any man can love a woman, and I always will. The Lord's been good to me and sent Glory Ethel in the sunset of my life. I love her, too. But that won't change a thing between us." He chucked her under the chin. "You're my wonderful one-and-only Jersey Queen."

She threw back her head and laughed.

"There. That's more like my girl."

Her laugh became a chuckle. "Papa, how is it that you can always make me laugh, even when I'm feeling blue?"

"Because that's the way it is between us, Molly, and that's the way it will always be." He patted her hand. "Now, how about Florence?"

"I'll be there."

He grinned. "I knew you would all along."

Molly stood up and put her hands on her hips. "Wait until I tell Glory Ethel what a con artist you are. She might be just the woman to give you your come-uppance."

"I'll bet she could, too." He shook his head, grinning. "Sakes alive, what a woman!"

The next morning Molly stood at her window, staring out. It was Thursday. She knew because she had checked the newspapers, and looking at the paper had reminded her of Samuel. He was gone now. She felt it. The house felt empty, the neighborhood felt empty, the town felt empty.

She pressed her nose to the glass and watched the street. If he passed this way, she'd spot him. His was the only Rolls-Royce Silver Cloud in town. Would he pass by? Robins Street was not on a direct path to Florence,

Alabama; but still, one never knew. Maybe he would stop to say goodbye.

She stayed with her nose pressed to the glass for fifteen minutes. Patience was a part of her everyday life. She'd spent hours being still, posing while an artist worked with his brushes and his oils.

No Rolls-Royce Silver Cloud went down the street. No brooding dark-eyed man passed her way. In spite of that, in spite of the fact that he was probably miles away from Tupelo by now, she felt the pull, felt the connection.

She turned from the window and stared, unseeing, as Mickey and Minnie pranced into the room. "Ahh, Samuel. What have you done?"

Samuel and Glory Ethel were back in Florence by midmorning. He'd been quiet on the ninety-mile trip, and so had Glory Ethel.

He parked in front of the Victorian house on North Wood Avenue.

Glory Ethel turned to him in the car. "Are you coming in, Sam?"

"Not today. I have a lot of work to catch up on."

"You *will* be at the party."

"Of course."

"Why don't you come and stay in your old room next week, help me get ready for the big shindig?"

"Won't the Rakestraws be staying with you?"

"Yes. But the house is big enough for all of us."

He stared off into the distance, seeing not the wide green sweep of oak trees along the street but a woman with golden hair and turquoise eyes. "I'm not even sure this town is big enough for all of us."

"What did you say? I can't hear you when you mutter."

He turned around and patted her cheek. "Never mind, Mother. I'll unload your bag."

He unloaded her suitcase and escorted her into the spacious, polished hallway of her house.

"You will stay here, won't you Sam? It'll do you good to get away from that lonely apartment."

"I'll think about it." He kissed her cheek. "'Bye, Mother."

After he left his mother's house, his first stop was the bank. He'd unload his bag later. Business came first.

He went straight to his office on the top floor and checked with his secretary about priority phone calls and mail. Then he went down the hall to talk with Carmondy, one of his vice presidents and his top operations officer.

Carmondy, just back from a vacation in Paris, was looking fit and rested and happy.

"Come in, Samuel."

Carmondy was a backslapper and always greeted everybody in a jovial manner. It wasn't Samuel's way, but he didn't mind as long as Carmondy got the job done.

"It's good to have you back, Carmondy."

"You, too, boss. Enjoy Tupelo?"

Samuel was just about to reply when he saw the painting propped on the wall beside Carmondy's wall. It was enormous. It was shocking. And it was Molly.

She was reclining on an array of red silk cushions, her long perfect legs stretched out, and her hair making a curtain of gold down her bare back. A length of red silk bared one breast and angled down her stomach, draping artfully across her hips. The artist had captured the wicked, wanton look in her turquoise eyes; the come-touch-me texture of her golden skin; the pouty, just-loved look of her perfectly sculpted lips.

"Astonishing, isn't it, Samuel?"

Samuel stared at the painting. He was incapable of words.

Carmondy took his silence as homage due the beautiful woman on his wall.

"When I saw that painting in Paris—it was in a little gallery near the Louvre—I fell in love, figuratively speaking, of course. My wife was mad enough to die when she found out I'd bought it. She wouldn't let me hang it in the house, so I sneaked it down here today." Carmondy laughed, very much at ease as his boss walked closer to the painting. "I guess I can drape it with a curtain until I decide what to do with it. Looking at it does tend to distract—"

"Carmondy! Let's talk business." Samuel spun on his heel and walked away from the painting toward a chair beside Carmondy's desk. He was totally unaware of the look on his face. It was enough to quell a stampede of elephants.

Carmondy was undaunted. Everybody knew the boss was all business. He cheerfully pulled out his chair and opened a folder on his desk.

"Right, boss. Business first, women later."

Samuel didn't even smile.

Samuel couldn't get the painting out of his mind. He avoided Carmondy's office for the rest of the week, sending his secretary back and forth between them if he needed anything from his chief operations officer, or relying on the telephone.

Over the weekend he moved temporarily into his mother's house to help her with party preparations. By the time the day of the party arrived, his nerves were ragged and his temper was on edge.

He purposely stayed at the office late so he'd miss the arrival of Jedidiah and Molly. Mostly Molly. He thought if he could just get through the party and the wedding, he could put her out of his mind and get on with the business of preserving the family fortune and the family reputation. Though how he would explain a stepsister who posed naked was beyond him.

The house was quiet when he slipped inside. He could smell the roses Glory Ethel had arranged all over the house. It was like some damned funeral parlor. Crystal and silver glowed in the light of the chandelier, and hors d'oeuvres and petit fours and every frivolous food ever invented were laid out on the dining-room table— enough to feed five hundred, he'd guess. His mother never did anything in a small way.

Nobody was in sight. He supposed they were all getting dressed for the party, or, knowing his mother, out trying to buy a whole hog, complete with an apple in its mouth, to put in the center of the table.

He went grimly up the staircase and started down the hall to the room that had been his since his childhood. Halfway down the hall, the door to his sister's room opened, and out stepped Molly.

Every ounce of Samuel's blood rushed straight to his head. He stopped dead still.

Molly was wearing a dress that bared so much flesh she might as well have been naked. She was a feast for the eyes, and he devoured her like a starving man.

Molly, coming so unexpectedly on Samuel, was equally mesmerized. Joy surged through her and she smiled. But when she saw the look on his face, the smile quickly died. She stood in the doorway, torn between giving him a warm hug and ducking back inside without saying a word.

They stared at each other so long that she could almost hear the minutes dragging by. She suddenly felt hot, even in the dress that she had deliberately chosen for comfort in the sweltering heat of the old Victorian house.

A ceiling fan lazily stirred the humid air above their heads, and in the depths of the house, they could hear the rattling of the ancient air-conditioning system as it strained to deal with the excessive heat of July in the Deep South. Still, neither of them spoke.

Molly shifted her weight and the strap of her dress slid slowly downward to bare her right shoulder. The sight spurred Samuel to action.

He strode across the small space that separated them and gripped her shoulders.

"Where in the hell did you get that dress?"

Molly's head snapped back and her eyes flashed. "Is it customary to greet guests that way in Florence, or is that your idea of good manners?"

"Good manners be damned! I asked where you got that dress."

"From my closet. It's filled with frocks designed to drive bankers mad."

Samuel had a sudden vision of Carmondy's face, his lust for Molly as clear as if it had been stamped there in red ink. Samuel's rage boiled over.

Holding Molly's shoulders, he backed her into the room and kicked the door shut. She glared up into his face, defying him, taunting him.

"I charge more if you insist on using caveman tactics."

"This is no time for your jokes, Molly. Get out of that damned dress."

"You didn't say 'Pretty please.'"

"You will *not* wear that dress to this party." He released her and stomped across the room to the closet.

"What do you think you're doing?"

He jerked open the door and began to rummage inside. "I'm getting you a decent dress." The coat hangers rattled in alarm as he shoved them around. "Bea is bound to have something suitable hanging here."

"Suitable! Suitable for what? A wake?"

"Suitable for polite Florence society. While you're here you *will be* suitable, or you'll have me to deal with."

"How dare you!"

He found what he was looking for and turned around, holding the dress in a death grip.

"This is my house and my town, and I won't have you doing anything to jeopardize everything I've worked for during the last twenty years."

"Just who do you think you are, barging in here and ordering me around? I'm a grown woman and perfectly capable of deciding what I will or will not wear." Molly had never been so angry in all her life. She had come to Florence somewhat reluctantly, but she had been willing to keep up appearances for Papa's sake. All that had gone by the wayside now. Samuel was giving orders as if he owned all of Florence and half of Alabama. She wasn't about to knuckle under.

Being told what to do always brought out the worst in her.

She raked her hand through her hair, lifting it seductively off her neck. Then she shrugged her shoulders so that her other strap slide down her arm.

"What's the matter, Sammy baby? Afraid you'll lose me to some good-looking local hunk?" She batted her eyelashes at him. "Why, honey chile, I'd be more than willing to give the Florence boys a thrill."

He tossed the dress onto the bed and pulled Molly into his arms. He enfolded her against his chest, forcing her to tilt her head backward. She glared straight into his eyes.

"Don't you ever let me catch you playing games with the men in this town. Is that clear?"

There was more in his face than anger. There was pain—a hurt buried so deeply that only someone with Molly's compassion could see it. That look took the edge off her anger. But she would be darned if she would let him order her around about the dress.

"It was not my intention to play games, Samuel. I chose this dress because I wanted to stay cool."

Suddenly all the anger drained out of him, and he felt shame. Never in all his life had he treated a woman—or anybody else, for that matter—with such high-handed tactics. He loosened his grip on her shoulders.

"Did I hurt you, Molly?"

"No."

"You're sure?"

"Yes," she whispered. A languor stole over her, and her blood flowed richly through her veins, pulsing in her throat like a trapped hummingbird.

They stood that way for a small eternity as shock waves of awareness swept over them.

He traced the plunging neckline of her halter dress, letting his fingers linger on her soft, silken skin. Then he moved them slowly upward to rest on the pulsing at her throat.

"I'm sorry, Molly. I don't know what got into me."

"Nerves. I'm feeling a bit on edge myself."

His smile was crooked and heartrending. "Don't be too generous with me. I can't promise not to do this again."

"Why, Samuel?"

With agonizing slowness, he swept his fingers gently over her throat, around her jawline and upward into her hair. Lifting the heavy strands, he let them sift back through his fingers.

"You bring out the beast in me."

She struggled against the magic of his touch, fought against the connection that wound them more and more tightly together.

"Funny, I thought it was only the tyrant."

"That, too."

He watched the shining hair fall through his fingers. The urge to bury his face in that fragrant cascade was so strong he had to clench his jaw to keep from giving in.

Unconsciously he leaned closer—so close he could feel her warm breath fanning his cheek. His gaze lingered on her lush lips, and the memory of her kisses made his breathing ragged.

"Samuel..." Her lips parted, as inviting as a dew-kissed rose.

Mentally he shook himself like an old wet dog. He couldn't afford to be bewitched by Molly. Especially not tonight, of all nights.

He released her quickly and picked up Bea's dress. "Don't make this difficult, Molly. Please just wear the damned dress."

She took the garment from him. It was a sedate black dinner dress, expensive and elegant and about as exciting as last Sunday's casserole. It was also about her size, judging from the looks of it.

"Your sister has good taste."

"Thank you."

She tossed the dress onto the bed. "But it's not *my* taste, Samuel." She pulled her shoulder straps up and smoothed down the hem of her bright coral party dress. "You'll just have to hold your head up somehow, and pretend that I'm perfectly suitable for polite Florence society."

He looked pained. "I didn't mean to sound so pompous, Molly. I just want this party to go smoothly."

"I can promise you that I won't swing from the chandelier or dance on the tabletops or even flirt with the local swains. I think I can survive one evening without those activities. But I *am* wearing this dress."

The only time he'd ever seen such a stubborn look on a face was when he'd been twelve and Beatrice had been eight. He'd had a new baseball and glove and had gone off to play backlot baseball with the boys in his neighborhood. Bea had tagged along. Not only that, but she'd insisted on playing the game. When he had told her girls didn't play baseball, she'd stuck out her lip and said she'd prove that girls could play better than boys. And she had. She'd hit two home runs that afternoon.

"I'll concede the victory to you." He gave her a mock bow. "But don't expect to win every time."

"Does this mean we're going to fight a lot?"

"Probably. But I've come to find our little skirmishes stimulating."

She propped her arms on the ornate brass footboard of the bed and grinned at him like a naughty child. "You might even find a few of them educational."

"Is that a warning, Molly?"

"No. It's a promise."

He cocked one eyebrow at her. Molly, in a stubborn mood, was extraordinarily beautiful—and desirable. But then he'd discovered that Molly in any mood was intoxicating. And having her leaning on the bed didn't help matters one bit. He decided that in the future it might behoove him to stay out of the bedroom when he confronted her.

"I'll see you downstairs at the party." He started toward the door, then stopped and said over his shoulder, "And, Molly, I'll be watching to see that you keep your promise."

She chuckled. "I never break promises, Samuel."

The sound of her laughter followed him out the door. It was going to be a very long evening. He strode quickly to his room and began to dress.

After he left, Molly put the finishing touches on her makeup and hurried down the stairs. She'd heard guests arriving for the last ten minutes and she didn't want to miss a single thing. Now that she was in Florence and her first encounter with Samuel was over, she was feeling perky and ready to party. She didn't know what she had expected—perhaps the tenderness that had so undone her in Tupelo. Or maybe she had expected another of those soul-searing, possessive kisses. Expect for that heady moment when he had held her in his arms, she had come through their encounter all in one piece. And she had won their skirmish. She had promised to be good, of course, and she would; but not *too* good. Too good was boring.

She was smiling when she stepped into the festive living room downstairs.

Glory Ethel came across the room and kissed her cheek. "You take my breath away, you're so beautiful." She glanced up the staircase. "Have you seen Sam, yet?"

Molly's face flamed. "Yes."

Glory Ethel took note of the flushed face, but wisely refrained from comment. "Good. He works so hard, I wasn't sure whether he would even take time off for the party." She took Molly's hand and patted it. "My dear, would you mind keeping an eye on him? He's been an absolute bear this week. I don't know what's wrong with him."

"I'm sure he'll be fine. Anyhow, I'm not exactly the chaperone type. I—"

Glory Ethel cut her off. "Here he is now." She turned toward her handsome son, who was descending the staircase. Taking Molly's hand, she dragged her over. "This sweet thing has agreed to look after you, Sam." She linked their hands. "Now, you behave and don't give her any trouble."

Glory Ethel departed in a swirl of chiffon skirts and a cloud of perfume. Molly couldn't help but smile. Papa was *very* lucky.

"You can take that wicked smile off your face, Venus. I didn't intend to be looked after."

She faced him, and quickly wished she hadn't. At close range, Samuel Adams in a tuxedo was deadly. This was one time she dearly wished she was a coward and able to run. Instead, she thrust out her chin.

"You needn't put any more gray hairs in your head worrying. I have more important things to do than watch you."

"Shall I make a few wild guesses, or do you intend to tell me?"

She looked about the room, taking her time. She wanted to madden him as much as he maddened her.

"Well, the chandelier appears too flimsy for swinging. And there's too much food on the table to have any dancing room." She paused long enough to zero in on the handsomest man in the room. Actually, the next handsomest. And he finished a poor second to Samuel Adams. "But I do see a local swain who is pining for me to give him a thrill."

"Venus, I'm warning you...."

She tossed her head and laughed. "I remember. You make people quake in their boots. But you should remember, too, I'm not wearing boots." She reached for the hem of her skirt.

Samuel's hand snaked out and caught her wrist. "Save those legs for a more appreciative audience."

Her smile was a study in wicked innocence. "You don't appreciate them?"

He ignored that taunt. "A *private* audience."

"Tsk, tsk. Have you forgotten? The whole world is my audience."

Carmondy's picture floated through his mind. "Florence, Alabama, is not the whole world. And don't you forget it." He left her abruptly and stalked toward the table. He knew it was a retreat, but it was the best he could do at the moment. Dammit, the woman was driving him crazy.

He took a glass of champagne from the table and raised it to his lips. He hated champagne, but he downed the entire glass in three swallows. Across the room, Molly was flirting with Graden Williams—by George actual flirting. Rage obscured his vision for a moment, and then he reined himself back under control. What did it matter what she did? She'd be in Florence for only a day or two, anyhow; and then she'd return to Tupelo or Paris or wherever the hell she had to go and pose naked.

He clipped another glass from the table, more to have something to do with his hands than anything else. They kept wanting to curl into fists and smash something—mostly Graden Williams's smirking face.

Samuel made his way across the room, stopping occasionally to chat with friends, smiling and nodding to others as if he were enjoying the evening, playing the role of perfect host. But all the while he was moving closer to Molly. His mother had gotten their roles reversed. *She* was the one who needed looking after. As head of the family, it was his job to take care of her.

When he was close enough to overhear their conversation, he stopped. Still holding a full glass, he leaned against a marble column Glory Ethel's decorator had insisted on installing in the room, and watched Molly. She had already besotted poor hapless Graden. And it had taken her less than ten minutes.

Samuel began to see the humor of the situation. He relaxed and decided to enjoy the entertainment.

"Gra-den, don't tell me you do all that by yourself? You run a whole de-part-ment store? How fa-sci-nating."

Samuel grinned. Molly's exaggerated drawl was so thick it could be swirled around a fork and still not drip on the plate. He was amazed that Graden didn't see through it. But then, Graden had probably never met a woman like Molly.

For that matter, neither had he. His mother had an earthy humor and a big laugh, but she was as plain as yesterday's meat loaf. His sister Bea was beautiful, of course, but not in an ordinary way. Bea's was a subtle beauty that would go unnoticed unless you took the time to really look at her. She was not at all like Molly.

He lifted the glass to his lips and watched her over the rim. Her vibrant, vivid beauty socked him in the gut, and he found himself holding his breath. Since he'd spotted that painting in Carmondy's office, he couldn't look at Molly without picturing that perfect, lush body of hers. Her clothes didn't help a bit. He felt as if he were looking right through them. He must be losing his mind.

Giving a snort of self-disgust, he turned to go. But Molly's next words stopped him.

"Well, Graden, I'm *certain* Glory Ethel's garden is lovely this time of year. I'd be de-lighted to take a stroll in the moonlight with you."

"We might even find something besides flowers, Molly girl."

Over his dead body. Samuel squeezed the champagne glass so hard the stem popped. Champagne cascaded to the floor and the top half of the glass shattered against the tiles. Samuel caught the sharp eye of a waiter, gave a peremptory nod, put the rest of his glass on the waiter's silver tray, and then zeroed in on Molly.

He took her arm and smoothly drew her to his side.

"There you are, my dear. I thought I had lost you."

"How can you lose me, Samuel? You never had me." She tried to pull her arm free, but he held it in a tight grip. "Anyhow, I can't talk to you now. I'm going for a moonlight stroll with Graden." She gave him a spunky grin and kicked his shin.

He didn't even grunt. Instead he smiled at her like a benign father. "I'm very sorry to interrupt your plans, but we do have important business to discuss." He favored Graden with one of his best president-of-the-bank glares. "You *do* understand, don't you?"

Graden knew enough about Samuel Adams not to cross him. "Certainly. Anyhow, I need to give my con-

gratulations to the happy couple and be on my way. Tomorrow is a big day at the store." He backed off.

"Nice seeing you Graden. Thank you for coming."

Molly kicked his shins again. "Let go of me, you big
tyrant."

"My dear, if you kick me one more time, I'll be forced
to kiss that smile off your face."

"You wouldn't dare."

"Wouldn't I?" That dangerous eyebrow of his
quirked upward.

"Of course not." She cocked her head to one side so
she could see his face better. "Besides, you can't do two
things at one time."

A hint of a smile played around his lips. "And what
is that other thing I'd be doing?"

She took her time, smiling innocently up at him, wid-
ening her eyes in a way she'd been told drove men mad.

"I think showing is so much nicer than telling, don't
you?"

"It depends on who's doing the showing and what's
being shown."

"Oh, I'm doing the showing, Samuel. This is *my*
game." She hooked her arms quickly around his neck
and stood on tiptoe. She'd expected at least a token show
of resistance, but he just stood there, grinning at her.
No, not grinning: leering, smirking. Not that exactly,
either. What he was doing was looking at her like some
big jungle cat who has just seen his dinner.

Her heart hammered against her rib cage, but she
pressed on. She slid her hands up the back of his neck
and tangled them in his hair. He still hadn't moved. His
smile made her shiver.

"I'm waiting, Venus. Are you going to show me?"

She lost some of her courage. She knew she should go ahead right then with her plans. Strike while the iron was hot, and all that business. But Samuel was such an intimidating man. She wavered just a moment too long.

Suddenly she found herself being lifted off her feet.

"What in the world are you doing?"

He slung her over his shoulder, caveman style. "Relax, my dear. This will be painless."

"You put me down!"

"Why, Venus, I thought you were the one who loved excitement?" He strode across the room, taking his time, smiling and nodding at the guests, even stopping to chat with a few while she hung upside down over his shoulder.

"She's feeling a little faint, Herb. I'm taking her out for air."

"No, she's not sick, Mrs. Reims. She just loves to be carried around this way."

"You know how it is with women, Clyde. They have to be shown who's the boss every now and then."

Molly hammered her fists into his back. It was useless. He continued his relentless march toward the French doors.

"Tyrant." She tried to kick the fronts of his knees, but he caught her legs in a vise grip and pressed them tightly against his body.

"I warned you about playing with fire. Remember?"

How well she remembered. But she wasn't sorry. Not one bit. As a matter of fact, she hadn't had this much fun since she'd jumped into the fountain at Pierre's party on the Left Bank in Paris. She'd get him for that remark about showing women who was the boss, though. All she had to do was wait for an opportunity. And it would come. She knew that as well as she knew she was Venus de Molly.

Samuel reached the French doors and pushed them open. A blast of humid summer air smote them. Molly's thin dress immediately went limp. Samuel felt as if he were melting inside his tuxedo.

"This damned heat," he said.

Molly took heart from his words. They were the only indication that he wasn't as in control as he pretended to be. She relaxed against his shoulder and enjoyed the ride across the well-lit, stone-paved patio, through the rose garden and into the darkness of the trees.

When they reached the shelter of a magnolia tree, he stopped. Putting both hands on her waist he lowered her to her feet. He took his time, pressing her tightly against his body so that she felt every sizzling inch of him. She was glad for the darkness. If he had seen her face, he'd have known exactly how much he was disturbing her.

"Now, what was that you were going to show me, Venus?"

At the moment she couldn't have shown him the Tennessee River if it had been rolling over her feet.

He chuckled. "Lost your nerve, my dear? In that case..."

He bent over her, blocking out the moon, the stars, the deep velvet sky—blocking out everything until there was only his face with its piercing black eyes and its ruthless mouth.

Chapter Six

Molly braced herself. She knew he would capture her lips as swiftly as a nighthawk captures his prey. A part of her longed for the kiss, hungered for that particular brand of passion that only Samuel Adams could provide; but another part of her fought the attraction.

When his face was only inches from hers, she found the will to speak. "I'm so glad you showed me how to act in polite Florence society."

Her words brought him to a halt. He stared down at her for a second, and then suddenly he laughed. At first it was a small chuckle, and then it became a full-bodied roar of mirth. Still holding on to her shoulders, he threw back his head and gave vent to his joy.

When his laughter subsided, he smiled down at her. "Molly, do you think I'm so straitlaced that I never have any fun?"

"I don't know, Samuel. Do you?"

Her question burned through his mind as he watched the play of moonlight across her face. Did he? Until he'd met Molly, his life had consisted of work and responsibility and an occasional outing with a suitable woman. But fun? The fun had stopped when he was fifteen and his father abandoned the family. No, his life had not been fun—not until Molly. But he couldn't tell her that. At least not now—not until he'd had some time to think about it.

"I've had my share of fun, Venus. But there is a difference between fun and scandal."

Any other time, she would have seen the pain in his eyes and she might have made the connection between his obsession with scandal and the loss of his father. But she was in too much emotional turmoil to be discerning. Samuel was pulling at her heartstrings in ways she couldn't handle.

She tossed her head back and glared at him. "And you think I'm scandalous. Is that it?"

For a brief instant his face softened, and she thought he would deny her accusation. Instead, he released her shoulders, stepped back and leaned against the trunk of the magnolia tree.

"Venus, you're the most scandalous woman I've met since . . . in a long, long time. And quite frankly, I don't want you as a member of this family."

His words hurt, but she didn't let him see that. "I'm not too thrilled with you, either. But I'm willing to make the sacrifice for Papa."

It was a long time before he spoke. He studied the stubborn tilt of her chin, the proud bearing of her body. She made him ache in a way that no woman had ever done. It was more than desire, more than passion, more than a need for physical release. He ached to share the joys of her spirit and know the depths of her mind. He ached to caress her and comfort her and shield her. For Molly Rakestraw, he ached to make the world a perfect place to live.

He felt like a cad for hurting her. And he had. In spite of her brave comeback and proud bearing, he knew that his words had wounded her.

He reached out and put his hands on her shoulders. "Molly, let's go back inside to the party."

The tenderness of his touch and in his voice surprised her. Shivers crawled over her skin, and for a moment she couldn't move, couldn't speak. She could only stand and feel the warmth of his hands upon her bare skin.

"Aren't you afraid I'll scandalize you?" she whispered.

"You won't have the chance, my sweet." Releasing her shoulders, he tucked her hand through his arms and started back toward the house. "I intend to keep you at my side for the rest of the evening."

"I can think of worse punishments."

"So can I." He stopped in the rose garden and looked down at her. "Don't tempt me, Venus."

"Sir Adams the Bold, you're the last man in the world I want to tempt."

Her declaration was heartfelt, and if he thought it was because she wasn't attracted to him or didn't even like him very much, that was fine with her. He need not know that it was self-protection.

With so much misunderstanding separating them, they went back inside to the party. Samuel worked through the crowd with the ease of a man who is very much at home in a social setting. Occasionally he risked letting go of Molly's arm, but not often—especially not when he caught a wicked gleam in her eye. For the most part he kept one arm draped casually around her shoulders or wrapped possessively around her waist.

Glory Ethel was the first to notice. Standing beside the punch bowl with Jedidiah, she watched her son with interest. He was more relaxed than she had seen him in a long, long time, and when he looked at Molly... Glory Ethel put her hand over her heart and sighed.

Jedidiah leaned close. "Did you say something, sweetheart?"

She patted his hand. "No, dear. It was just a sigh of contentment."

"You *are* happy, aren't you?"

"Yes. For all of us." She gazed across the room at Sam and Molly once more.

Jedidiah glanced that way. "The children look happy. I just wish your daughter could have been here too."

"She'll be at the wedding."

The party broke up shortly before ten. Samuel kept Molly at his side until the last guest had departed. Glory Ethel and Jedidiah briefly passed their way to say goodnight. Claiming they were getting old, they went down the hallway to separate quarters on the first floor.

"You can let go of my arm now."

Samuel had held on to Molly for so much of the night that it was no longer a conscious action on his part. He released her quickly, and was surprised at how empty his hand felt.

"Right. The party's over."

"And I didn't do a thing socially unacceptable."

Guilt slashed him. "Molly, not only were you socially acceptable, you were extraordinarily charming. I think half the people who came are now fans of yours."

IT'S FUN! IT'S FREE!
AND IT COULD MAKE YOU A
MILLIONAIRE

If you've ever played scratch-off lottery tickets, you should be familiar with how our games work. On each of the first four tickets (numbered 1 to 4 in the upper right)—there are PINK METALLIC STRIPS to scratch off.

Using a coin, do just that—carefully scratch the PINK STRIPS to reveal how much each ticket could be worth if it is a winning ticket. Tickets could be worth from $5.00 to $1,000,000.00 in lifetime money.

Note, also, that each of your 4 tickets has a unique sweepstakes Lucky Number...and that's 4 chances for a BIG WIN!

FREE BOOKS!

At the same time you play your tickets for big cash prizes, you are invited to play ticket #5 for the chance to get one or more free book(s) from Silhouette. We give away free book(s) to introduce readers to the benefits of the *Silhouette Reader Service™.*

Accepting the free book(s) places you under no obligation to buy anything! You may keep your free book(s) and return the accompanying statement marked "cancel." But if we don't hear from you, then every month we'll deliver 6 of the newest Silhouette Romance™ novels right to your door. You'll pay just $2.25* each—and there's no charge for shipping and handling!

Of course, you may play "THE BIG WIN" without requesting any free book(s) by scratching tickets #1 through #4 only. But remember, the first shipment of one or more book(s) is FREE!

PLUS A FREE GIFT!

One more thing, when you accept the free book(s) on ticket #5 you are also entitled to play ticket #6 which is GOOD FOR A VALUABLE GIFT! Like the book(s) this gift is totally free and yours to keep as thanks for giving our Reader Service a try!

So scratch off the PINK STRIPS on all your BIG WIN tickets and send for everything today! You've got nothing to lose and everything to gain!

 Here are your BIG WIN Game Tickets, worth from $5.00 to $1,000,000.00 each. Scratch off the PINK METALLIC STRIP on each of your sweepstakes tickets to see what you could win and mail your entry right away. (See official rules in back of book for details!)

This could be your lucky day - GOOD LUCK!

TICKET 1
Scratch PINK METALLIC STRIP to reveal potential value of this ticket if it is a winning ticket. Return all game tickets intact.

LUCKY NUMBER

1H 558689

TICKET 2
Scratch PINK METALLIC STRIP to reveal potential value of this ticket if it is a winning ticket. Return all game tickets intact.

LUCKY NUMBER

3P 560331

TICKET 3
Scratch PINK METALLIC STRIP to reveal potential value of this ticket if it is a winning ticket. Return all game tickets intact.

LUCKY NUMBER

5M 558454

TICKET 4
Scratch PINK METALLIC STRIP to reveal potential value of this ticket if it is a winning ticket. Return all game tickets intact.

LUCKY NUMBER

9S 557837

TICKET 5
We're giving away brand new books to selected individuals. Scratch PINK METALLIC STRIP for number of free books you will receive.

AUTHORIZATION CODE

130107-742

TICKET 6
We have an outstanding added gift for you if you are accepting our free books. Scratch PINK METALLIC STRIP to reveal gift.

AUTHORIZATION CODE

130107-742

YES! Enter my Lucky Numbers in THE BIG WIN Sweepstakes and tell me if I've won any cash prize. If PINK METALLIC STRIP is scratched off on ticket #5, I will also receive one or more FREE Silhouette Romance™ novels along with the FREE GIFT on ticket #6, as explained on the opposite page. (U-SIL-R 07/90) 215 HAYS

NAME _____

ADDRESS _____ APT. _____

CITY _____ STATE _____ ZIP _____

Offer limited to one per household and not valid to current Silhouette Romance™ subscribers.
©1990 HARLEQUIN ENTERPRISES LIMITED

PRINTED IN U.S.A

FOLD AND DETACH ALONG THIS DOTTED LINE—RETURN ALL GAME TICKETS INTACT.

Carefully
detach card
along dotted
lines and
mail today!

Play
all your
BIG WIN
tickets
and get
everything
you're
entitled to—
including
FREE BOOKS
and a
FREE GIFT!

She checked his face to see if he was sincere. Satisfied, she smiled. "You know, Samuel, you can be quite nice when you're not trying so hard to be a bear."

"Is that what I am, Molly?"

"Sometimes. A great big grizzly." She watched changing emotions flit across his face. Reaching out, she touched his cheek. "But sometimes..." Her fingers played briefly across his skin. "Sometimes, you're nothing but a big teddy bear."

His smile was bittersweet. "Then I'll have to watch myself. I can't be getting soft in my old age."

"Indeed not. You have your reputation to think of." She withdrew her hand. "Good night, Samuel."

"Good night, Venus."

He stood in the hallway watching her while she ascended the stairs. She never looked back. When she reached the top, he turned quickly and strode out the front door. He had to get away.

His Rolls-Royce purred to life and he drove through the darkened streets of Florence. He passed the University of North Alabama campus and Trowbridge Sandwich Shop. He drove through the city, past McFarland Park, until he came to the river. Crossing the Tennessee he realized that driving wasn't enough. He needed physical activity to exorcise whatever demons were haunting him.

Across the river he turned up River Bluff and headed toward his private health club. Thank God he had a key and after-hour privileges. He parked outside underneath a hundred-year-old oak and let himself in. Jerking off his tie and jacket, he went straight to his locker.

For the first time in his adult life, he didn't bother to hang up his clothes. Tuxedo pants and shirt and coat and tie were strewn across the floor. He dressed quickly, pulling on the first pair of athletic shorts he could get his hands on.

Taking his ball and racquet, he went straight to the racquetball court. He took careful aim and smashed the ball viciously against the wall. The sound echoed through the empty health club. Samuel drove himself, concentrating only on the ball and his target.

Sweat poured off his brow and slicked his chest. After forty-five minutes of punishing activity, he sat down to catch his breath. A vision of Molly rose up to mock him. He saw her in her kitchen with a tear on her cheek; he saw her under the magnolia tree with moonlight gilding her hair; he saw her laughing in the slatted swing with mud on her face.

"Dammit." He straightened and slammed the ball against the wall. It didn't help. Molly was still on his mind and in his heart.

He let the racquet drop to his side and took a deep, steadying breath. It was getting late, and tomorrow he had a bank to run. He didn't have time to stand around the health club till midnight like some besotted fool—like Taylor Adams.

He stalked over to his locker, jerking up his scattered clothes as he went. Then he climbed into his Rolls-Royce and headed back to the house on North Wood Avenue.

The windows were all dark. At least no one would see him, sweaty and exhausted and out of sorts, climbing the stairs, dressed in his gym shorts and, for Pete's sake, his tuxedo shirt. He didn't know why he had felt it necessary to put on a shirt for the drive home. The streets were empty, anyhow. For that matter, he didn't know why in the hell he hadn't just gone back to his apartment.

His steps slowed as he passed Molly's bedroom door. For an insane moment he thought he smelled her fragrance. What had she called it? *Night of a Thousand Splendors.* He almost groaned aloud. Only a door separated them. All he had to do was put his hand on the doorknob and turn. She would be there, stretched out on his sister's brass bed, her hair spread across the pillow, her long, lovely legs gleaming in the moonlight.

The old wooden floor creaked as he took a step toward her door. What in the hell did he think Molly would do if he walked into her bedroom? Throw her arms around him and drag him into her bed?

Shaking his head in disgust, he walked quickly down the hall to his own room. He didn't bother to turn on the light. He knew every stick of furniture in the room and exactly where it was placed.

Without turning, he tossed his tuxedo pants toward an easy chair.

"Mfft."

Samuel whirled around at the sound. An apparition rose from the chair. One delicate hand gleamed in the moonlight as it reached up to push aside his tuxedo jacket. A familiar face came into view.

"Molly! My God. What are you doing in my room?"

"Waiting for you." She tossed the jacket onto the chair with her right hand and untangled the trousers from her left. She took her time with his clothes, acting as serene as if she had come to his room for Sunday-afternoon tea.

When she had added his pants to the pile of clothes on the chair, she faced him.

"Why don't you turn on the lights, Samuel?"

"Is there any particular reason I should?"

"I don't like to work in the dark."

They faced each other across the darkened room. She was outlined by the pale strip of moonlight that shone through the windows. He could see that she was still wearing the same dress she'd worn at the party. Desire gripped him so tightly he had to grit his teeth to keep from groaning.

He sought to regain control by moving toward a floor lamp. "A pity. I do some of my best work in the dark." He turned the switch, and lamplight illuminated her face. She didn't look as much at ease as she sounded. That was good. He was in no condition to handle Molly in top form.

He stepped out of the pool of light and watched her.

"You're not wearing trousers."

"Do I need pants for this game you're playing, Molly?"

"They would have been nice, but gym shorts will do." She looked down at his legs. The tuxedo shirt completely covered his shorts. "You *are* wearing gym shorts, aren't you?"

"Why don't you come over here and find out?"

She caught her lower lip between her teeth and assessed him. She'd thought it would be easy. While she'd waited for him to return, she'd planned the whole thing. But she hadn't counted on his being half dressed and looking as if he had already whipped sixteen mountain lions and was eager to whip sixteen more. Nor had she counted on her own feelings.

Her gaze swung to the bed. It seemed to loom larger as she looked at it. She hadn't bargained on how she would feel in his bedroom. She felt hot and languid and flushed and excited and altogether in no condition to deal with Samuel standing half naked and looking like an avenging god.

But she was determined to carry out her plan.

"You have the most wonderful ideas." She started slowly across the room.

"Has anyone ever told you how sexy your walk is?"

She slowed for half a heartbeat, then continued her walk. "No."

"They should have."

"Perhaps you need to give all my suitors lessons."

"I have a better idea."

"What?"

"Come closer and I'll show you."

Things weren't working out the way she had planned. Samuel was supposed to be feeling trapped. He should be retreating. But she'd come too far to back out now. Plucking up her courage, she took the last few steps toward her target.

"Why don't you let me show you, Samuel?" She made her voice a sexy purr as she reached for his shirt.

Samuel steeled himself against her touch. He would not let her see how close she was to being thrown across his bed. He refused to let any expression on his face or action on his part let her know how much he wanted to bury himself in her soft flesh.

Her hands were working the top stud of his tuxedo shirt now. He had a decision to make. He could let her continue her game, or he could put a swift stop to it.

He studied her. She was tense, ill at ease and uncertain. He was intrigued. What was she up to? Finding out would be amusing.

Silently she removed the top stud from his shirt, taking great care not to make too much contact with his skin.

Samuel tried not to smile.

"Do you need some help, my dear?"

Her eyes were wide as they swung up toward his.

"No. I can handle this myself." Her hands fumbled and she dropped a stud on the floor.

"I can see that."

She ignored the barb and the stud on the floor. She'd show him who was the boss. Taking a slow, ragged breath, she reached for the next stud. She could do it. It was just a matter of pretending.

A trickle of sweat rolled between her breasts as she unfastened Samuel's shirt. He was ominously silent. Why didn't he say something? Why wasn't he doing anything? She wanted to peek up to see if she could read his intentions on his face, but she dared not. Now that she was set on her course, she didn't need anything to distract her.

When all the studs were removed, she set them on the bedside table. Putting that small distance between herself and Samuel gave her time to recover.

The room was silent except for the metallic sound of tuxedo studs pinging against wood. Molly took her time, gathering her courage to face Samuel again.

"Your back presents a lovely view, my dear. Do you intend to stand beside my bed for the rest of the evening?"

She whirled around to face him. He wasn't laughing, but she could see the amusement dancing in his eyes.

"No. I have other plans."

She marched bravely back across the room. His tuxedo shirt gleamed impossibly white in the lamplight, and where it gaped, she could see portions of his chest. Taking a deep breath, she caught the front of the shirt and pulled it open.

Sweat sheened his skin and glistened on the dark hair that swirled across his chest. Slowly she pushed the shirt aside and put one hand on his chest. He felt damp and solid and electric. She had meant to be bold and to drive him wild with her caresses, but it took all her willpower to keep from jerking her hand off that powerful chest and running.

His heart pulsed beneath her palm, and the sound of her own breathing was harsh in the room. Her hand trembled.

Suddenly he chuckled. It was a deep sound of gratification.

"That's a great start, Venus. What next?"

She tilted her head so she could look directly into his mocking eyes. She'd be darned if she'd let him get the best of her.

"Do you really want to know, or shall I just show you?"

"Surprise me, Venus. Show me."

"Don't say you didn't ask for this." She slid his shirt down his shoulders, intending to toss it carelessly on the chair. Unfortunately the shirt didn't cooperate. And neither did he. Samuel stood still while she struggled to get the sleeves over his hands.

She was so flustered she wanted to kick something—mainly him.

"I think you forgot the cuff links."

"What?"

"The cuff links. They're still in my shirt."

"I knew that. I was just testing to see if you did."

"Naturally."

He chuckled again. Laughter was his only defense. The minute she'd touched his bare chest, he'd been lost. He knew that if he reached for her now, if he caught her in his arms and captured those inviting lips, there would be no turning back. The web she was beginning to weave around his heart would become chainlinks, and he'd be bound to her forever.

He watched intently as she removed his cuff links and put them on the bedside table. If he didn't know better, he'd think that she had never done this before, that she had never gone to a man's bedroom for the specific purpose of seducing him.

Seduction. That was her game. And she seemed to be a novice at it. He was foolishly glad.

When she came back to him she seemed calmer, more sure of herself. She slipped his shirt quickly from his shoulders and tossed it onto the chair; then she leaned down and kissed his bare chest, right over his heart.

Shock waves washed over Samuel. There was a harsh sound, and he realized that he'd been the one to make it. It was a groan of pure animal longing. Quickly he brought himself back under control.

"That's not so bad for a beginner, Venus."

Her head jerked up. "How did you... I'm not a beginner."

"Prove it."

She stared at him for a full minute, and then she smiled. The smile dawned slowly, like a sleepy sun that had almost forgotten to make his appointed rounds. Her smile widened until it dazzled him. He almost wished he could call back his challenge.

Molly hooked one arm around his neck, while the other made slow circles on his chest.

"How do you like your women, Samuel? Sweet and slow? Or fast and wicked?"

"Are you giving me a choice? How refreshing."

"That's part of my charm."

She dipped her head down and put her lips on the side of his throat. It was a sweet touch that made him shiver.

Suddenly her tongue flicked out and moistened his skin. He instinctively reached for her. Warning bells sounded in his mind. His hand wavered and then withdrew. In his condition he couldn't afford to touch her—not even one hair on her head.

He gazed down at that rich golden hair and he knew pain. Not gathering her to his heart caused an ache that was almost physical. But doing so would have brought certain heartbreak.

He stood very still and endured.

She lifted her head to look up at him. Her eyes were wide with question.

"That was nice, Venus."

"Nice?"

"If you expect effusive praise, you'll have to do better than that."

"I plan to." She took a deep breath. "Why don't we move to a place that's more comfortable?"

"You'll have to be specific, my love. I'm new at this."

Darn his wretched hide, she thought. He was deliberately making this as difficult for her as possible.

She wet her lips with the tip of her tongue. "The bed."

"You'll have to speak up. I didn't quite catch that."

"I said . . . *the bed*."

The words echoed around the room like a cannon shot. Samuel stifled his laughter.

"That's what I thought you said." He started nonchalantly toward the bed, and then, as if it were an afterthought, he reached for her hand. "You might as well come, too, since this was your idea."

Anger was beginning to take the place of uncertainty. Molly had never seen a more arrogant man in her entire life. He deserved everything she planned to do to him.

"I'll be glad to, but it would be so much nicer if you would carry me."

Her sudden courage intrigued him. And he began to have his suspicions that this was more than a seduction.

"I'm happy to oblige, my dear." He swept her into his arms and deliberately pulled her hard against his chest. The move forced her head onto his shoulder. "Comfortable, Venus?"

"Very."

He smiled. "You're sure you want to do this?"

"Absolutely."

"That's what I love. A willing woman."

He strode toward the bed and lowered her to the mattress. She made a move to sit up, but he was faster. Catching her wrists, he brought them over her head and held her down. With one knee propped on the bed, he leaned close.

"Changed your mind already, my sweet?"

His eyes were fierce and bright, but she met him stare for stare. Sweat glistened on his bare chest, and a damp trail of perspiration made the bodice of her dress cling to her. They both noticed. Her hands itched to caress his slick bronze skin, and he longed to bend down and kiss away the moisture on her satin cleavage.

"No," she whispered. "Have you?"

He held her down a moment longer, studying her.

"You were made to grace a man's bed, Molly." Abruptly he released her.

Molly lay back against the pillows and placed her hands over her hammering heart.

He lifted one of her hands to his lips. "Feeling shy, my love? Perhaps I can help you." He turned her hand over and planted a lingering kiss in her palm.

When she could trust herself to speak, she pulled her hand away. "I don't need any help."

She sat up and smoothed her tumbled hair back from her face. They faced each other on the bed, like two jungle cats stalking each other.

"Why don't you..." Her voice was only a whisper. She stopped and tried once more. "Why don't you lie back on the pillows?"

He obliged, grinning. "You like to be on top? My dear, you keep surprising me."

Even lying down, he still looked as if he were capable of doing battle with Goliath. And his skin! It was slick and bronze and delicious and dangerous. She'd have to touch him soon or abandon her game.

Leaning down so that her hair shielded her face, she stilled her trembling hands and ran them over his chest. She heard his sharp intake of breath. So far, so good. Still keeping her curtain of hair between them, she slid her hands into the waistband of his gym shorts. He offered no resistance as she lowered them down his legs.

He was wearing sexy briefs. She tried not to look, but her eyes kept straying in that direction. Her effect on him was painfully obvious. She bit her lip and tossed his shorts onto the chair.

"Your hands are soft."

She jumped at the sound of his voice. Her head swung around, and she stared at him. He was no longer laughing. A muscle pulsed in his tightened jaw, and his eyes were as dark and deep as the pits of hell.

"A model has to take care of all parts of her body, including her hands."

"Is the rest of your body as soft as your hands?"

She couldn't speak.

"I could find out." He made a move to rise.

"Don't."

"It's your game, Venus."

He was making it easy—too easy. But she didn't question her good fortune. All she wanted to do now was finish her work and get out of his bedroom.

Moving quickly, she reached into a pocket of her shirt and pulled out two lengths of red silk ribbon. She took one of his hands and lashed it to one of the bedposts.

"Intriguing, my dear."

She didn't reply. Biting her lip, she leaned over him and tied his other hand to the opposite bedpost.

The sound of his laughter echoed around the bedroom. He wasn't supposed to be laughing, darn his ornery hide. She'd give him something to laugh about.

Feeling bolder now that he was tied down, she bent over and reached for his briefs. He shivered when she touched him. She'd never known that touching a man in such an intimate way would make her feel like this—triumphant and uncertain, all at the same time. There was something mysterious and magical about that unseen, untouched flesh below a man's waistband.

Molly's fingers tingled and her palms felt sweaty. Biting her lower lip, she began to inch his briefs downward. There was no sound in the room except his harsh breathing. Her hands clenched involuntarily, and she pinched his smooth, forbidden skin. His back arched, and all she could see was the dark swirl of hair on his flat stomach, intriguing, silky-looking hair that disappeared into his briefs.

She closed her eyes. There was a small sound in the room, a low moaning, as if the night wind had crept under the windowpane and sighed with pleasure.

"Did you say something, my dear?" Samuel's voice was soft and wickedly seductive.

Molly's eyes snapped open and her head jerked up. A flush heated her cheeks as she realized that *she'd* made the sound. That wouldn't do at all. She had to control herself. She had to finish the game.

"I was just clearing my throat."

"That's what I thought you were doing, my love. Carry on."

He stretched, and she'd swear that he wiggled his hips just to spite her. She squeezed her eyes shut again and grabbed his briefs. Nothing was going to stop her. She jerked, and the darned ornery things got stuck. It was like trying to peel a banana whose skin had been glued to the fruit. She hadn't counted on that. Ignorance was not bliss at all: it was embarrassment.

Sweat popped out on her brow, and she tried again. She felt his hips lifting, and the offending garmet slid free. That wretched, arrogant man had actually *helped* her. She was too relieved to care.

With her eyes still closed, she got off the bed. She felt a little light-headed, and had to grasp a bedpost for balance. She drew two quick breaths, then opened her eyes and headed for the safety of a chair across the room. She carefully avoided looking at the bed.

His wicked chuckle followed her all the way. She sat down in the chair and gripped the arms.

"How does it feel to be my captive, Samuel?"

"Why don't you look and see how it feels?"

She forced herself to look at him. She'd have to do it eventually, anyhow. Samuel Adams, naked on his bed, was an awesome sight. How he could manage to look like a warrior god with his hands tied with red silk ribbons was beyond her. But he *was* tied up. She'd have to remember that.

She smiled at him. "Every now and then, men have to be shown who's the boss."

"Is that all you're going to do? I'm disappointed."

"Perhaps this will make you feel better." She picked up a sketchpad and a pencil lying beside her chair. She worked quickly, relying on her memory, sketching Samuel's dark hair and Roman nose and sensuous lips. Next she drew the broad chest. She didn't have to look at the bed to see it. It was forever etched in her memory.

He looked at her bent head. The silky golden hair lay against one very pink, very flushed cheek. That appealing aura of innocence glowed about her. He lay against the pillows, content to wait a while longer. And to watch.

"The naked body is a work of art, Samuel."

"It's also a very efficient machine, designed for work . . . and for love."

"You still think it belongs only in the bedroom?"

"Yes."

"I'll show you." She looked up from her sketchbook to get the exact fluid line of hip and leg. His body mocked her. So did his smile.

She bent over her work again and quickly finished the sketch. It was a talent she'd learned from the street artists in Paris. When she'd finished, she stood up and tore the drawing from the sketchpad, making a loud sound in the quiet room.

She waved the sketch in the air. "Here's the evidence, Samuel. Your body is a work of art."

"Thank you, my dear."

"I don't want your thanks. I just want to change your bullheaded mind."

She placed the drawing on a table beside the chair and turned to leave the room. Behind her, there was an ominous tearing sound, then footsteps.

"Did you think I was your captive, my dear?"

Samuel's large hand gripped her shoulder, and he spun her around. She could see the torn ribbons dangling from his wrists.

"What are you doing?"

"Never underestimate your opponent, Venus."

His mouth came down on hers. The kiss was fierce and wild and hungry. Every ounce of passion he'd kept in check through the nerve-racking party, through the vicious game of racquetball, and through her tantalizing seduction was finally released.

He dragged her hips into his and pressed against her filmy chiffon skirt. He wanted her to feel the power and danger in him. He wanted... Oh, God! She felt so good. He wanted to lower her to the floor and find release.

He kept her in his bruising embrace a while longer—mainly to prove to himself that he could kiss her and walk away. When he let go, he noticed that her lips were red and her eyes were extraordinarily bright. She looked incredibly desirable.

He hardened his heart.

"Go back to your room before you get into trouble." He turned her toward the door. "*Real* trouble."

Chapter Seven

She hurried from the room, closing the door softly behind her. When she reached the hallway she leaned against the wall. Her ordeal was over. And what had it proven? Certainly not that she could ever get the upper hand with Samuel Adams. And certainly not that they would ever see eye-to-eye in the matter of the body as art.

She closed her eyes, and the memory of his sizzling kiss washed over her. Oh, Lord, he was a dangerous man. His arms had been divine, his kiss heaven. Wrapped in his embrace she'd willingly have walked off to the ends of the earth.

She struggled with the temptation to go back to his room and climb into his bed. What would it be like to share that big four-poster with him? What would it be like to make an irrevocable commitment to Samuel Adams?

Suddenly she pictured a mound of earth in a wind-swept, empty corner of the cemetery—hard red clay as cold as death. She shivered. The struggle between her heart and her will ceased, and she walked slowly back to her bedroom.

Samuel was gone when Molly awoke the next morning. It was just as well. She didn't think she could have faced him after that scene in his bedroom.

She and Jedidiah spent a happy, busy day with Glory Ethel, planning the wedding. And late that evening, they sat down together in the big house on North Wood Avenue and prepared to eat dinner.

There was an empty place at the table.

"Is Samuel coming to dinner?"

Molly thought her question was innocent. She had no idea how bright her cheeks and eyes were.

Glory Ethel noticed, and silently approved. "I never know about my son. He told me not to plan for him, but still, a mother can hope."

Molly squelched her disappointment and changed the subject. "You have a wonderful name. Do you mind telling me how you got it?"

"I was the last of nine children, eight of them boys." Glory Ethel paused to laugh. "Land, how my daddy did want a girl. When the doctor told him that I'd been born, he rushed into Mama's room and shouted, 'Glory, Ethel, it's a girl!' As if she didn't already know." She wiped tears of laughter from her cheeks. "The name stuck."

Jedidiah reached over and caught her hand. "The name suits you. You are my glory woman."

"And you're my sweetheart, Jedidiah." She patted his hand. "I can't wait for Bea to meet you."

"What's she like?" Molly asked.

"The spitting image of Samuel—dark hair and dark eyes, like their daddy. And twice as stubborn. Land sakes, that woman thinks she can run the world with one hand tied behind her back. And she nearly can, too. I don't know where my two children got all their gumption."

Two of them in the family. Two arrogant, bossy, dictatorial... Memories of last night intruded on her thoughts. Handsome, powerful, sexy, delicious...

"Molly."

She jerked her attention back to the present. "Yes, Papa?"

"Glory Ethel asked if you'd like to live with us. You've been talking about leaving Paris and setting up your own little gallery. You could have your choice of towns. We'll keep both houses, sort of go back and forth as the mood strikes us."

"That's sweet of you, but I won't be here much longer. After the wedding I'm going back to Paris."

"I thought you were going to take a long vacation, Molly. You deserve it."

"I had planned to, Papa. But models can't drop out of sight for too long or they'll be forgotten. I need to go back." *Have to go back,* she added to herself. She had to put an ocean between herself and Samuel. And then she wasn't sure that would be enough.

Molly had been gone from Florence for two days. Samuel had avoided seeing her since that night in his bedroom, four days ago. It seemed like only four minutes. The taste and touch and smell of her was still with him.

He slammed shut the file folder and opened his desk drawer. Molly's sketch lay on top of the telephone directory. He picked it up for the thousandth time and studied it. He was no fool. What he was seeing was not a picture of a naked man but a nude study. It was art.

Molly was good. And she was right: the unclothed human body didn't belong merely in the bedroom. Done in good taste, it belonged in museums and art galleries and even on office walls.

He put the sketch back into his drawer and buzzed his secretary.

"Delores, get Carmondy down here."

It took Carmondy only five minutes to get to his boss's office. Samuel Adams didn't like to be kept waiting. He sat in the chair facing Samuel's big desk and snapped open his briefcase.

"You won't need that."

Carmondy didn't ask questions; he simply closed the case.

"What's up, boss?"

"That painting in your office. I want to buy it."

"It's not for sale."

"Everything can be had for a price. How much?"

Carmondy wasn't afraid of arguing with Samuel. His boss was bright, tough and hardworking, and he expected all his employees to be the same. But he also expected and encouraged them to use their own judgment and to speak their mind.

Carmondy started to state again that the painting was not for sale, and then he took a closer look at Samuel's face. It was as fierce and determined as ever, but it was also haunted, as if he were seeing a vision that he couldn't quite believe.

"You really want that painting, don't you, Samuel?"

"Yes. How much?"

"Well, I'm going to be blunt with you."

"That's what I expect."

"I'm crazy about it, but my wife Martha isn't too taken with it. She won't let me hang it at home, and to be honest with you, it doesn't quite fit the image of a staid old bank—even draped in a curtain." Carmondy chuckled. "You can have it for exactly what I paid for it."

"Done."

"I guess you'll want to pick it up in the next day or two."

"I'll send Wayne for it immediately."

Wayne, Samuel's sometime chauffeur and sometime housekeeper and all-the-time gofer, did his usual efficient job. By the time Samuel reached his apartment that evening, the painting of Molly was hanging on his bedroom wall.

He tossed his briefcase onto a chair, loosened his tie and stretched out on his bed. Propping his hands behind his head, he studied the painting.

Molly smiled down at him. She teased him and taunted him. She made him feel good and kind and warm and generous. She made him feel strong and protective.

Everything that was good in him rose to the surface. To his absolute astonishment, he realized that he was in love with Molly. He rose from the bed in alarm. That could never happen to him; he was far too wise for love. Love made fools of men.

He paced the floor, glancing up every now and then at the painting. Molly smote him in the chest like a blow. No amount of reasoning could counteract his deep gut instincts. Molly Rakestraw, aka Venus de Molly, was the woman he had to have, the woman he had to make his own.

"Marriage," he muttered. "Good Lord, we're talking marriage now." He continued his restless pacing, wrestling with the problem, viewing it from all angles. As a businessman he was accustomed to looking for the bottom line, and the bottom line was simple: he was in love with Molly.

He analyzed his options. An affair was logical. He could have Molly; and then when he came to his senses, they would both be free. He stopped beneath the painting and gazed at it, and he knew beyond a shadow of a doubt that he could never let her go. Whatever the risks of marriage, whatever the potential for pain, he had to have Molly on a lifetime basis. Commitment, marriage, family—the entire package.

He stood studying the painting, expecting a trapped sensation to come. Instead, he felt nothing except joy. He threw back his head and laughed aloud.

"Do you know what you've done, Venus de Molly? Do you have any idea what you've done to this dyed-in-the-wool bachelor, this polite, scandal-avoiding citizen?"

Wayne stuck his head around the door. "Did you call for anything, sir?"

"No, Wayne. I'm just talking to myself."

"Talking to yourself, sir?"

"It's a new habit I've acquired."

"Yes sir." Wayne turned to go.

"Wayne..." Sam said. The older man turned back. "Thank you for hanging this painting."

"Did I put it in the right place?"

"It's perfect."

Wayne gave him a grin that showed two gold teeth and then limped back down the hall. It occurred to Samuel that Wayne was getting too old to drive. He'd have to hire someone else and call him Wayne's assistant. The old man had his pride.

He turned his attention back to the canvas. Only three more days until the wedding and he'd see Molly in the flesh.

He could wait—barely.

Glory Ethel and Jedidiah had a home wedding just at sunset. It was nothing fancy—just the two of them with their children and a few friends in the gracious parlor of Dan and Janet Albany's huge house on Church Street in Tupelo.

Samuel didn't make any pretense of listening to the wedding ceremony. He stood in front of the flower-banked mantel with his mother and gazed across the way at Molly. She stood like a vision. She was wearing another of those moonbeam dresses that made his throat dry.

He caught her eye and smiled. She smiled back, but it was not the kind of smile that made a man want to do handstands of joy. Sam was not deterred. His chance was coming soon.

The minister pronounced Glory Ethel and Jedidiah man and wife. They linked arms and joined their friends for the wedding celebration.

Moving quickly, Samuel took Molly's arm. She looked as if she might protest, then she clamped her mouth shut and allowed herself to be escorted. He led her through the wedding guests and straight out of the parlor. Still holding her arm, he guided her into a small book-lined study and shut the door. His briefcase was on

the desk where he had put it that morning after he and
his mother had arrived from Florence. They had come
straight to the Albany house—some fool notion about
the bride not seeing the groom till the wedding. One of
Dan Albany's baseball caps hung on the back of a chair,
and a stuffed lamb belonging to one of the Albany twins
lay on the floor beside the chair.

"What on earth do you think you're doing?" Molly
reached for the doorknob.

He put one hand on the door and held it shut. "I've
brought you in here for a private talk."

"I don't want to talk to you."

"That's obvious. You've avoided me since I arrived in
Tupelo this morning."

"I was busy this morning." She reached for the doorknob. "We should join our parents."

"They'll never miss us. At least not for a while."

She looked so fragile standing there, so innocent, so
young. She was young. Twelve years younger and less
experienced than he. He'd have to remember that.

He reached out and tenderly cupped her face, tilting
it up to his.

"Molly, look at me." His thumbs caressed her jawline. "I know you're probably still thinking of our con-
frontation in my bedroom."

Her blush told him he was right.

"It worked, Molly." Her eyes widened. "That's right.
I'm completely convinced that you are right about art. I
was wrong."

"What is this? Some new scheme of yours to gain
control? Some new plot you've hatched to tame me?
Right?"

"Wrong. What I'm trying to tell you . . ." He paused and laughed at himself. "Oh, God, I didn't know I'd be so bad at this."

"Bad at what?"

"Molly, will you come and sit with me on the sofa? I want to tell you a story."

She looked askance at the leather love seat. She didn't relish the idea of being cooped up with Samuel any longer; she was afraid her heart would betray her. But he *did* look sincere and somehow vulnerable.

"I'll stay five minutes longer. Only five minutes. And then I'm going back to help Papa and Glory Ethel celebrate their marriage."

He released her and led her to the love seat. Resisting the urge to pull her into his arms, he watched as she sat as far away from him as the small sofa would allow. He couldn't help but remember the day they'd met. He could still picture her in the slatted swing with the sun shining in her hair. How bold she'd been then! He didn't want her to change, and he certainly didn't want her to be intimidated by him. That was quite an admission from someone who had spent most of his life controlling other people.

"Molly, when I first learned of my mother's intentions to marry your father, I was very much opposed."

"You thought we were after your money."

"I'll admit that the thought crossed my mind. Primarily, though, I was opposed because of you."

"You've made that perfectly clear."

"I was wrong, Molly."

He saw the play of emotions on her face—astonishment, acceptance, joy. For the first time since he'd entered the room, he felt hope. He seized the opportunity to press his case.

"You are the dearest, most joyful, most charming woman I've ever met, and I was crazy to believe that having you in the family would be anything except a pleasure."

She wanted to believe every word he had said, but she forced herself to be cautious.

"That's quite a pretty speech, and I believe at least half of what you said."

"Which half?" He smiled.

"The part about me being charming. I like to be thought of as charming."

Never had the urge been greater to take her into his arms. But he'd come too far to jeopardize his future with a wrong move.

"You certainly are."

"Thank you."

"You're more than welcome." He allowed himself the pleasure of lifting her hand to his lips for a brief kiss. She shivered. He considered that a good sign.

He lingered over her hand, but when she gave the slightest tug, he released it.

"Molly, I'd like you to know why I was so determined to keep you out of my family."

"You don't have to justify your reasons to me, Samuel. You've admitted that you've changed your mind, and I'll accept that. We can be friends."

"I want us to be more than friends.... I want us to be lovers."

Anger colored her cheeks bright pink. She rose from the sofa with all the dignity of a wounded goddess. "I should have known that all your pretty speeches were just another ploy to manipulate me."

She stalked toward the door, then turned for a last word.

"I wouldn't climb into your bed if you were the last man on earth."

Four days ago he would have pulled her into his arms and kissed her until she didn't have the will to resist. But not now. She was too important to him. He sat on the love seat and watched her walk out and slam the door.

"Dammit." He stood up and fought the urge to smash his fist into the wall. He wasn't accustomed to failing, and he'd failed royally with Molly. Furthermore, he hadn't even told her what he'd intended to say. The only excuse he had for his failure was that he was totally inexperienced in dealing with a woman he loved.

He'd had women, lots of women. But they had meant nothing to him except pleasant companionship for the occasional evening of entertainment. He guessed he had a hell of a lot to learn about being in love.

Lovers. My God, he had asked her to be his lover. One look at her, and he'd completely forgotten his careful plan of wooing and winning and proposing.

He wondered how long he could sit on the sofa and nurse his wounds. About three more minutes. Would Molly cool down in three minutes? He grinned wryly. Knowing her, she was probably planning another magnificent revenge.

When Molly left Samuel, she didn't even take the time to regain her composure. She marched back to the parlor in all her mighty splendor and rage. She pasted a brilliant smile on her face to cover her anger, and went straight to the table of champagne.

She picked up a glass and downed it in four gulps—and she didn't even like champagne. She set the empty glass down and picked up another. It was halfway to her lips when a woman spoke.

"Weddings do drive one to drink, don't they?"

Molly turned around to face one of the most gorgeous women she'd ever met. The woman had hair as black as patent leather, and big eyes so dark they seemed to be bottomless. She was wearing a sapphire silk dress, stunning in its simplicity.

The woman stuck out her hand. "Hi, I'm Beatrice Adams."

Molly took her hand. The grip was firm. "Molly Rakestraw."

Bea smiled. "Yes, I know. I came over here for the specific purpose of introducing myself to you."

"I'm sorry I didn't meet you earlier. I was almost late for the ceremony."

"I *was* late for the ceremony. Planes—you know how they are." She shrugged her elegant shoulders and lifted a glass of champagne from the table. "So...tell me what you think of this marriage between our parents."

"I'm proud for both of them. Papa and Glory Ethel are very much in love."

"I don't believe in love."

Good grief, Molly thought. Was it a disease in the Adams family?

"Then you and your brother have much in common."

"With good reason. Taylor Adams, our father, abandoned us when we were teenagers. All in the name of love."

Stunned, Molly set her glass down and reached for Bea's hand. "I'm so sorry."

"Don't be. Perhaps we're better off for having learned that lesson while we were still young." She studied Molly. "She was blond, like you."

Molly didn't have to ask who Bea was talking about. She released Bea's hand and picked up her own glass of champagne. "I don't mean to pry, but I think I can understand you and your brother better if I know more about your father."

Bea hesitated only a moment. "Since it's all in the family...he was a handsome man. Too handsome. That's what attracted Betsy Martin to him. That and his money. She'd come to The Shoals to cut a record—she was a singer. A really beautiful woman. Sexy, flamboyant—not at all like my mother." Bea's glance swung across the room to Glory Ethel. "My mother is the salt of the earth."

"She is. And I promise you that Papa will be very good to her."

"I intend to see that he is."

Molly's heart went out to Bea. She was trying so hard to be a tough, hard-boiled woman, but underneath she was just like any other human being—much in need of love and understanding.

"So do I."

For the first time since they'd met, Bea's smile was one of real pleasure.

"I like you, Molly."

"I like you, too, Bea. I think we can be very good friends."

Bea laughed. "If you're satisfied with a friend you see only on major holidays, it will work."

Samuel came back to the party in time to see Molly and his sister laughing together. He went straight to them.

"Bea, it's good to see you laughing."

Bea turned toward her brother. "How could I not, around Molly? She seems to have a gift for laughter."

She caught her brother around the shoulders and gave him a hug. "How are you, Sam?"

Samuel gazed over the top of her head at Molly. "I'm better now than I've been in years."

Molly stared back. *Why didn't you tell me, Samuel?* she thought. *Why didn't you tell me from the very beginning that I reminded you of the woman who stole your father?* She wanted to reach out and cuddle him against her breast, and then she remembered what he'd said a moment ago. *I want us to be lovers.*

She set her glass on the table and walked away.

Samuel watched her leave. He released Bea and began to answer her rapid-fire questions, but his mind was on Molly. She was across the room now, hugging his mother and her father, giving them that radiant smile he knew so well.

Molly stayed with their parents while he and Bea discussed their mother's future. Then Molly moved out of his line of vision. He had to maneuver around Bea under the guise of getting a glass of champagne in order to keep Molly in his sight.

She was standing beside Janet and Dan Albany now, laughing and playing with the Albany babies, twins Richard and Katherine, if he remembered the names correctly. God, Molly was a natural with children.

"What are you grinning at? You look like those syrupy ads of doting fathers watching their daughter's graduation." Bea swung her head around to see for herself. With a look of disbelief, she turned back to her brother. "Molly?"

"You caught me red-handed."

"That's what you get for having a brilliant sister. How bad is it?"

"Very bad. Or very good, depending on your point of view. I'm in love with her."

Bea's face went white. She touched his arm and squeezed. "Just be careful, Sam. Please. I don't want to see you hurt."

"I can handle it, Bea. Don't worry about me." He studied Molly across the room. It was a long time before he spoke again, and when he did, his voice was filled with quiet conviction. "She's the one you should worry about. God, Bea, I'd rather die than hurt her."

"You won't."

"How do you know?"

"Because you're not like *him*."

Samuel didn't have to ask. Bea was talking about their father.

He lifted his glass of champagne to his lips. "Pray that I'm not."

He caught sight of a movement out of the corner of his eyes. It was Molly leaving the room. He set down his champagne glass and followed her.

Chapter Eight

Molly had to have air. She suddenly felt stifled by the wedding celebration.

She knew the Albany house nearly as well as she knew Papa's house. It was a marvelous mixture of classy elegance and interesting memorabilia. A Waterford vase shared space on a Victorian hall table with an ancient one-eyed teddy bear. Farther down the hall and through an archway, a huge watercolor of a fanciful carousel presided over an 1860s walnut table.

Molly usually enjoyed the house as much as she enjoyed the company of its owners, but not today. She paid scant attention as she made her way to the backyard.

Escape. That's what it was. But she didn't care.

Outside she headed for the tire swing in a corner of the fenced-in yard. Harvey, the Albanys' mixed-breed mutt who was napping under the oak tree, lifted his huge head, yawned and then went back to dreaming. Lying contentedly by his side, the poodle, Gwendolyn, didn't even bother to spare Molly a glance.

"Everybody I see is paired off—even the dogs," Molly muttered to herself, and stopped to kick a twig that had blown off the tree. She fitted herself into the tire swing, not bothering to be careful with her dress. Then she pushed her feet against the ground to shove off. There was something exhilarating about flying through the air—a freedom, a sensation of being young and carefree.

She closed her eyes, swinging back and forth, waiting for the feeling to come.

"If I were an artist, I'd paint you like this." Samuel caught the edges of the tire swing and brought it to a halt.

Molly turned to look over her shoulder. He was holding the swing so that when she turned her face was level with his. His eyes were alive with passion, and something else, too—something she couldn't put her finger on.

"Let me go . . . please."

"I'll never let you go."

"Samuel . . ."

He held the swing a moment longer, gazing into her face; then he gave it a gentle shove. Molly and the swing went soaring through the air.

"Do you like to fly high, my sweet?"

"Yes."

"I can take you high, Molly. Higher than you ever dreamed."

He gave the swing another push, but Molly knew that he wasn't talking about swinging. Her cheeks burned with the wind and with the ancient knowledge that rose within her.

When the swing came back down, Samuel caught it again and held it fast. Molly didn't turn, but she could feel his chest pressing into her back, his warm breath on the side of her neck.

"You smell like wind and wildflowers."

She didn't trust herself to speak.

He brushed his lips against the side of her face. "If I had two hundred years, it wouldn't be enough time to just look at you." His lips moved down along her throat and his voice grew husky. "It would take another five hundred merely to adore your face with my lips." His tongue tasted her skin. "To explore your body would take an eternity."

"Samuel . . . don't . . ."

"I must."

He circled her waist and plucked her from the swing. Pulling her back against him, he fitted her close to his body and buried his face in her hair.

She wanted to run, *knew* she should run; but she found it impossible to resist him . . . at least for the moment. With a sigh she leaned her head against his shoulder and closed her eyes, shutting out the oak tree, shutting out the evening sky, shutting out the Victorian house and its guests, shutting out everything except the pleasure of being in Samuel's arms.

"Ahh, Molly. Do you know how much I love you?"

She stiffened. "Love?"

His chuckle was soft. "I hadn't meant to tell you this way. I was going to woo you and court you and sweep you off your feet. I was going to bare my heart to you and teach you to love me." He turned her to face him. "Love is a strange and wondrous thing, Molly. Sometimes I think it makes fools of us all."

"Aren't you worried about shocking polite society with all that foolishness?"

"Not anymore. I don't know if I ever really was."

Molly softened. "Bea told me about your father. I'm sorry."

"It's in the past now. And that's where it's going to stay." He tipped her face up with one hand. "I don't blame you for being skeptical—not after everything I've put you through." He laughed with the sheer joy of being alive and bent down to kiss her stubborn chin. "We're going to be good together, Molly."

There it was again, she thought: that arrogant assumption that he could get exactly what he wanted by merely crooking his finger. She put her hands on his chest and shoved.

"You dictator."

"Molly..."

"Let me go, you barbarian." He released her, and she stood back, panting. "You couldn't get me to bed by telling me we were going to be lovers, and so you decided to try false professions of love. You blackguard. You stinker. You—" She paused for breath.

Samuel had always been a man of action, and he took action now. Pulling Molly into his arms, he kissed her. It was a thorough, no-holds-barred kiss. She fought him for four seconds, and then she decided the best resistance would be no response. That ploy lasted all of two seconds.

When he sensed her submission, he gentled the kiss until she felt as if she had floated off the earth and landed straight on a shining star. An absolutely glorious feeling stole over her, and she knew without a doubt that what Samuel had said was true. He *did* love her. And the knowledge scared her to death.

Her moan was one of pure agony. To love was to risk loss. And yet, not to love was to embrace a lonesomeness so great it didn't bear contemplation.

At last Samuel lifted his head and gazed down at her. "Molly, I love you. If I have to spend the rest of my life proving it, I will."

"You'll be wasting your time, Samuel. I'm not the marrying kind."

He whooped with laughter.

"I don't see anything funny about that."

"What's so humorous, my sweet, is that while I'm still thinking of the courtship, you've zoomed ahead to the marriage. I approve. We could get married and work everything else out at our leisure. Preferably in bed."

Dignity rose from her like steam from hot asphalt. "I would never consider you for a husband. You are totally unsuitable."

He smiled at her like an indulgent father. "Tell me, my sweet . . . what great failings do I have that made me unsuitable husband material?"

"Do you want me to name them all?"

"Be brutal, my dear."

"You're a dictator. I don't think you're fond of digging flower beds. I've never seen you act wild about dogs and babies. Your idea of fun is tossing me over your shoulder and parading me through a roomful of people."

"Anything else?"

"Well . . . I don't even know whether you like circuses and parades and chocolate sundaes with whipped cream and cherries, and wonderful theater with music that makes you laugh and cry, and popcorn with lots of butter on top."

"Why don't you find out?"

"Because..." She looked into his face and discovered that she couldn't walk away without telling him at least a part of the truth. "You have a life in Florence and I live in Paris, and I'm going home."

"You're going back to Paris? When?"

"My plane leaves tomorrow morning at seven."

It was a development Samuel hadn't counted on. Once he'd discovered he loved Molly, it seemed only natural to him that everything would work through to a logical conclusion—his way: commitment, courtship, and eventually marriage. And here was Molly, headed back to Paris on the next plane.

"Molly..." He touched her face—gently, like the caress of a hummingbird's wing. "Do you think that an ocean will keep me away from you? Do you think that distance will dim my love for you?" His hands moved across her cheek, memorizing its classic bone structure, cataloging its silky texture. "I'll follow you to the ends of the earth."

"Samuel Adams, you are the most stubborn man I've ever met," she whispered.

"And you are the most stubborn woman...and the most adorable. I love you, Molly...and someday you'll tell me that you love me. Someday very soon."

"Please..."

"Please what, Molly? Please kiss you? Please don't stop saying I love you?"

"Please let me go."

"I will—for a while. But first..." He bent his head and captured her lips once more. It was a kiss that Molly knew had been designed in heaven and sent directly by heavenly courier to this backyard on Church Street. She felt the brush of angel wings, heard celestial music, knew the glory of a spirit that soared.

The wonder of Samuel Adams saturated her, body and soul, and she trembled inside.

Finally he released her. "That was goodbye...for now."

She stared into space without speaking for a long while, and then she put two fingers over her trembling lips. "Goodbye, Samuel," she murmured. But he had already gone.

The evening darkness filled the void he had left behind and Molly knew the feeling of heartbreak. "What have you done to me, Samuel Adams?"

She slowly surveyed the yard as if she were seeing the landscape of a dream; as if she were trying to convince herself that the events of the last hour had really taken place. Her pain at his departure was great. What would it be like, she wondered, if she loved him, really loved him? To see him walk away, to put an ocean between them, or—heaven forbid—to leave him in some cold, forbidding spot of ground with nothing but a stone marker to tell that he was there...

She simply couldn't think about it anymore. Lifting her chin, she went inside to join the party.

Glory Ethel and Jedidiah were getting ready to leave on their honeymoon. Molly pressed forward for one last hug and kiss.

"Have fun, Papa...Glory Ethel. I love you. Both of you."

Papa patted her cheek. "Take care, sweetheart. Set Paris on its ear."

"I will, Papa."

Jedidiah escorted his new wife to the front door and they paused, laughing. Taking careful aim, Glory Ethel threw her bridal bouquet. Instinctively, Molly stuck out her hand to catch the flowers—a small nosegay of summer violets.

A cheer went up from the onlookers. The door clicked shut behind the newlyweds, and Molly turned back to her friends. Bea was leaning against the doorframe, looking elegant and somewhat aloof and slightly bewildered by all the commotion of the wedding. Janet and Dan Albany were saying goodbye to Glory Ethel's friends who had driven over from Florence. Jedidiah's friends were gathering their purses and walking canes and heading for the front door.

Samuel was nowhere in sight. Molly surveyed the room one more time just to be sure.

"Looking for someone, Molly?" It was Janet Albany who spoke.

"Not really."

Janet smiled and brushed a lock of hair back into her elegant chignon. "He's already gone."

"Who?"

"Samuel. Don't look so surprised. I saw him follow you into the backyard." Her smile was radiant. "Do you mind if an old friend gives you some good advice?"

"I'm pretty good at listening, but I'm not making any rash promises about following through."

"That's the spunky Molly we all know and love." Her laughter was happy and lilting, and caused her husband to gaze at her from across the room. Janet blew him a kiss, and he looked as if he'd won a million-dollar sweepstakes. "Three years ago, if anyone had told me I'd be married to a soccer coach and reducing my medical practice to part-time in order to raise my family, I'd have said they were crazy. I had at least a dozen good reasons not to fall in love. Fortunately, that wonderful man across the room changed my mind. I'm not saying that you should fall in love, Molly. I'm merely saying that if it happens to you and it feels right, don't fight it."

"Don't you ever get scared, Janet? Scared that it will all be taken away?"

"I'd rather have one moment with Dan and the twins than a lifetime guarantee that nothing would disturb my loneliness."

When she boarded the plane to Paris the next morning, Molly was still thinking of Janet's advice. It made a certain amount of sense—not that it mattered one way or the other now, for she was putting an ocean between herself and Samuel Adams.

She didn't want to think about him anymore. She reached for her headphones, selected some lively music and settled back in her seat to enjoy her flight.

Paris and Molly embraced each other like long-lost relatives. She strolled down the Champs-Elysées, stopping to smell the flowers and to greet old friends. She renewed her acquaintance with her favorites at the Louvre—the *Mona Lisa* and the *Venus de Milo*. She attended the Comédie-Française and the Opéra.

She went on a redecorating binge and turned her apartment upside down. She draped the walls with peach-colored silk and arranged silk floor cushions near the window that overlooked the park. She repotted all her plants, including the huge ficus tree that had stood in the same pot for the last four years.

Robin, her roommate, watched with an amusement that sometimes bordered on alarm.

"Molly." Spoken with his soft French accent, her name came out *Mollee*. "You make me dizzy with all this activity."

Molly looked up from the herbs she was planting in new hand-painted pots. "Just close your eyes, Robin, and think of all the wonderful gourmet meals you can cook using herbs from our very own windowsill herb garden."

"The plants look lively, the herbs sound great and the apartment walls look *marvelous*. It's you I'm worried about."

Molly put her hands to her cheeks, forgetting the dirt and streaking her face with potting soil. "Why? Do I look sick?"

"No. It's not the way you look that worries me, it's the way you act." He rose gracefully from the sofa, where he had been studying a book on cubist art, and crossed the room to Molly. He took one of her hands out of the potting soil, carefully wiped it off with a nearby tea towel, and brought it to his lips. After he had kissed the hand, he stuck it back into the pot. "You've been back two weeks now, and all you've said about your trip home was that it was *good*. I've heard you say more about the ads on the backs of cereal boxes."

"Well, it *was* good. Do you want me to tell you it was bad?"

"No. I want you to be your usual exuberant self. I want you to make me envy the parties you attended and long to meet the fascinating people you met." He looked down at the small herb she was potting, frowned and straightened it, then gazed back at Molly. "Did you meet someone, *chérie*?"

Molly had never lied to Robin. She saw no reason to start now. "Yes. I met someone. He's brash and handsome and passionate and tender, and he almost stole my heart." She laughed and waved her hand in the air. "But here I am, back in Paris with my heart intact."

For a moment she gazed into space and time and distance, seeing a black-eyed man whose touch had made her shiver, whose voice had turned her inside out. He'd declared his love for her, and yet she had heard nothing in the two weeks since she'd last seen him. She should be glad. That's what she had wanted—to put him out of sight and out of mind. Or was it? The memory of his kisses swept over her. She felt tears form in her eyes. How absurd! She would not cry. She blinked twice to stall the tears and then she smiled at Robin.

"Let's do something grand tonight, Robin. Let's go to the hottest night spot in town and be frivolous and carefree and wicked."

"I'd swim the Seine if it would bring back your dazzling smile. I know the perfect place."

"Is it wicked?"

"It's so wicked we could end up in jail."

"Good. I want to be shocking tonight. Very shocking." Her eyes began to gleam and she set her pots aside. "Robin, do you want to come shopping with me?"

"It's tempting, but you'll have to go without me, *chérie*. This afternoon I must work on a painting I've been commissioned to do."

She walked across the room and kissed his cheek. "Good luck." Then she picked up her purse and started for the door.

"You forgot something, Molly."

With her hand on the doorknob, she turned. "What?"

"You forgot to wash the dirt off your face."

For two weeks after the wedding, Samuel worked toward one goal—getting to Paris. While he was at the bank, he deliberately wiped Molly from his mind. But when he got back to his apartment at night, he indulged in dreams and fantasies and plans that made him restless. He'd never known that a day could seem like a year. But then, he'd never been in love.

All his efforts were directed at arranging his business so that he could take an extended leave. It wasn't easy. He wasn't the kind of man who flitted off to Paris, or anywhere else for that matter, at a moment's notice. Neither was he the kind of man who gave up control easily. He had endless sessions with his vice presidents before he was satisfied that the bank could run without him.

Finally, armed with information supplied by Jedidiah, he left Florence and flew to the City of Light, arriving in midafternoon. From Orly Airport he drove a rental car directly to a hotel near Molly's apartment.

He whistled while he unpacked his bags, then he picked up the phone and dialed her apartment. His assault had begun.

The nightclub on the Left Bank was crowded and cozy and smoke-filled. Candles stuffed into beer bottles and wall sconces behind the bar provided the only light.

Molly and Robin found a table and were immediately the center of attention. The club's clientele were primarily artists who either knew Molly or had heard of her. Many of them had painted her or sculpted her.

The nightclub resounded with their greetings. They crowded her table, talking and laughing, jostling for a place at her side.

Robin paid scant attention to the chatter. He brushed his sparse brown hair back from his thin face and gazed around the room. Nervous perspiration popped out on his brow. He hoped he was doing the right thing. He scanned the club again, searching.

There were two or three men who seemed to fit the description he'd been given over the phone, but suddenly he saw the right man. That had to be him, standing just inside the front door. He was tall and dark and he had the much-at-ease look of an American.

Everything was going to be all right, Robin thought. Relaxed now and feeling less like a traitor, he turned his attention back to Molly.

Across the room Samuel Adams stood just inside the club, waiting to let his eyes adjust to the dim light. His black eyes took in everything—the upright piano in the corner, the wizened guitarist seated on a stool beside the piano, the eighteenth-century walnut bar along the west side of the room, the nightclub patrons wearing such bizarre dress they might have been on their way to a costume ball.

Suddenly he saw her. *Molly.* She was wearing a turquoise dress that would sober skid-row bums. It was a tightly-fitted strapless gown, slit high enough to reveal one shapely leg all the way up to her thigh.

A man who had to be Robin was sitting beside her, watching every move she made with a mixture of fierce, almost paternal pride, and friendly concern. The other people were merely obstacles blocking Sam's path to Molly.

He strode across the room toward his target. The crowd at Molly's table took one look at his face and made way for him until he was standing behind her chair. She hadn't noticed him. Judging from the laughter of her audience, she was telling a very funny story—in French.

Leaning down, he placed his hands on Molly's shoulders. "Did you miss me, my sweet?"

She half rose from her chair, then sank back down. She thought she might faint, though she'd never been the fainting kind. *Samuel—in Paris!* her mind screamed. She made herself turn slowly to look up at him.

"Have you been absent, Samuel? I hardly noticed."

"Then we should remedy that."

He lifted her from her chair and kissed her, not caring that they had a huge audience. It was a bold lover's kiss. He held her so close, their bodies seemed to blend into one. When her knees went limp, he supported her, holding her upright as he continued his assault.

After it was over, he gently lowered her to a chair. She was speechless.

Smiling at the crowd around the table, he said, "She belongs to me."

A few understood and began to pound Samuel's shoulders in hearty congratulations. Robin, sitting across the table, translated for those who didn't understand English. They, too, joined in the celebration.

One of them, a big blonde who would have looked more at home in a wrestling ring than behind an easel with a brush, summoned a waiter and ordered wine.

"How dare you!" Molly accused.

Samuel pulled out a chair beside her and sat down. "My dear, I'm a busy man. I don't have time to stand in line behind all the local swains. I thought I'd stake my claim early."

"Stake your claim! I'm not a piece of property."

"No, you're not. You're a luscious, lively woman. And you're mine." He leaned over and kissed her cheek. "I'm here to make sure of that."

She pressed her trembling hands together under the table so he wouldn't see.

"How did you find me?"

"I can explain that." Robin spoke from the other side of the table.

"Robin? Not you?"

"I didn't mean to betray you, *chérie*. But when he called this afternoon..."

"While I was shopping?"

"*Oui, mon amie.* He seemed such a sincere gentleman...and you had been moping." He shrugged his shoulders. "I saw no harm in telling him where we would be tonight. I did what I thought was best for you."

Molly reached across the table in a quick gesture of compassion. "You always do, Robin...and there's no harm done." She smiled. "I can handle this."

Molly didn't turn to face Samuel immediately. She couldn't. While she pondered what to do, the wine was delivered and served. The crowd around her took their glasses and began to wander back to their own tables.

Samuel accepted a glass and drank silently. Molly could feel him watching her, waiting. All her senses were alert to him. A deep atavisitic longing stirred within her body. Her heart beat like the wings of a caged bird, fighting to be free. Her spirit soared with joy. But underneath it all, her strong sense of survival rose to the surface. She could not, *must* not, let this man establish claims on her heart.

She had to send him back across the ocean. And she knew exactly how to do it. Slowly she turned to face him.

"Molly," he drawled, "if your smile is any indication, you're up to devilment."

"Who? Me? Why, Samuel, how could you think that about your very own family?"

"How could I not, my dear? Your track record is fairly clear in that area."

"Then I suggest you go back to Florence. There's no need for you to stick around and witness my little indiscretions."

He lifted one eyebrow. "Little indiscretions, my sweet? How many men have you tied to your bed since you returned to Paris?" Her furious blush gave him his answer. His chuckle was low and satisfied. "None? I thought not." Leaning close, he gently caught her chin in his hand. "There will be no more men in your bed, Molly. Only me."

"I haven't . . ." She bit her lip to stop her own foolish confession.

"Innocence is not a sin, my love. It's a gift." He kissed her cheek and murmured in her ear. "I will be your first, Molly . . . and your last."

She couldn't answer him until the rhythm of her heart settled down.

"I suppose you want to get started right away." False sweetness and hard-won dignity oozed from her like thick honey.

He chuckled. "Not just yet, my love. I have to get over jet lag."

"Have you ever considered how hard it's going to be for an old man like you to keep up with a young thing like me?"

"I think you'll find me more than equal to the task."

"Good. I wouldn't want to hang out with somebody who would cramp my style."

"'Hang out,' Molly? Is that the same thing as making a commitment?"

"No. It means simply that while you're in Paris, I will consent to be seen in your company...as long as you can endure it."

"I think you'll find that my endurance is exceeded only by my stubbornness. I don't plan to let you go, Molly."

"I'll make you change your mind."

Leaning back in his chair, he smiled at her. "Carry on, my sweet. I'm going to enjoy every moment of this."

"Don't say I didn't warn you." She looked at Robin, who had been sipping his wine and avidly following their conversation. "Robin, would you be a sweetheart and ask the guitarist to play 'La Niña del Fuego'?"

"Not 'The Girl of Fire.' Molly, do you think this is wise?"

"Robin, have I ever let wisdom stand in the way of wickedness?"

There was no need to answer her question. Robin rose from the table and made his way toward the piano.

When the first haunting strains of the Spanish music sounded, Molly rose from her chair. Looking straight at Samuel, she smoothed her dress, stroking her body with slow, sensuous movements.

"Don't tempt me too far, Molly."

"Tsk. Tsk. Is your endurance already wavering?"

"No. But I'm making a remarkably quick recovery from jet lag."

Samuel had the satisfaction of seeing another blush stain her cheeks. Except for her high color, though, she appeared to be perfectly in control.

She tossed her gleaming hair over her shoulder and made her way toward the small dance floor. Moving directly to center, she began dancing. Lifting her hair above her head with both arms, almost as if she were stretching, she swayed in a lazy, undulating rhythm. The beautiful, eerie guitar music seemed to be pulsing within her.

Samuel watched her, spellbound. Her bright hair swayed with the rhythm, and her tight dress flared, revealing her long, luscious legs. Then the music became frenzied, wild. So did Molly's dance. Her movements were lusty and frankly sensual. A murmur rose from the crowd.

Sweat popped out on Samuel's brow. Need snaked sharply through his body. Slowly he stood, kicking his chair aside. His muscles were tense as he walked toward the dance floor.

Molly spun around and saw him. She never broke her step. Samuel lifted one hand high in the air, and she touched it with her palm. His feet stamped the hardwood while she whirled around him, her head back, throat bared, hips almost connecting with his, and then moving away.

A low "Ahh" sounded from the audience. The air vibrated with the sound of wild music and frenzied dancing.

Sweat dampened Molly's throat and trickled between her breasts. Her chest heaved with the physical exertion of the dance and her sharp awareness of Samuel. He moved with the grace and sureness of a panther, stalking his mate. His eyes were bottomless black, and his face was filled with passion.

Molly's breath caught in her throat as the guitarist struck his final, wailing chord. Samuel caught her around the waist with one hand and lowered her toward the floor, bending deeply over her.

She was limp and panting.

"I can never resist your invitations, my dear." His own breathing was ragged, and his hot breath fanned her throat.

She couldn't have replied if she were being threatened by a band of cutthroat gypsies. New sensations swamped her body. She wondered if the strange and wonderful feelings were the same as those of a woman who had just arisen from her lover's bed. Her face grew hot at the thought.

While the sustained chord hummed in the air, Samuel bent lower until his lips were touching her skin. She felt the abrasion of his tongue as it brushed against the side of her throat.

She moaned.

"Do you want more, my sweet? If you're looking for scandal, I can oblige . . . right here on the dance floor."

"Please."

His wicked dark eyes blazed down into hers, and for a moment she thought he was going to carry through with his threat. Finally he smiled and slowly lifted her upright. Then, taking her hand, he led her toward the table.

She didn't speak until she was seated.

"Where did you learn to dance the flamenco?"

"I dated a dance teacher once who thought it would be fun to teach me. I was hopelessly inept at the waltz and the foxtrot, but I seemed to have a knack for the Latin rhythms."

Molly had never known jealousy before, but she felt a sudden urge to cover the dance teacher with chunky peanut butter and set her out for the birds.

"Whatever happened to the teacher?"

"She married a stockbroker who didn't know a guitar from a goat." Samuel reached for her hand. Kneading her knuckles, he gazed into her face. "I intend to marry you, you know."

"So you've said."

He smiled tenderly. "Nothing you can do will change my mind." When she didn't reply, he added, "That was the point of the dance, wasn't it?"

"You hate scandal."

"You're not scandalous."

"Since when?"

"Since I fell in love with you."

There was nothing she could say to counter that statement. She looked across the table for a quick rescue from Robin. His chair was empty.

"Where's Robin?"

"He left with friends shortly after you started dancing. He said to tell you he'd see you in the morning."

"He wouldn't leave me like that. Certainly not with someone he hardly knows. Not with a stranger."

"I'm not a stranger, my love. I'm family... and I can be powerfully persuasive."

Of course, she thought. Robin would have known about the family connection the minute he heard Samuel's name. Before she left Paris, she'd told him all about going home to meet Papa's fiancée, Glory Ethel Adams. Anyway, she had called Samuel "family" a few minutes ago. Or had it been hours? She seemed to have lost all track of time.

"Molly... Look at me, my love." She turned back toward him and he caught her face between his hands. "There's no need to play games with me. I won't run away. I love you, my sweet. Don't you know that?"

"You keep telling me that."

"It's true. I'm not just saying that to lure you into my bed. I want more from you, Molly. I want commitment, marriage, children."

"I told you, I'm not the marrying kind."

"Why not?"

"Because . . . I'm too young."

Samuel could tell by the expression on her face that the reply was an evasion. He decided not to pursue the matter—at least not for a while. He released her and reached for the wine bottle.

"Would you like a glass of wine?"

"No. I'd like to go home."

"I'll take you. My rental car is outside."

"Samuel, that's the the first good news I've heard since you arrived."

He pulled back her chair and took her elbow. "It must be. Your smile is radiant." He led her across the crowded club. "I'm delighted that you think going home with me is such good news."

"That's not the good part. The good news is that you'll have two hands on the wheel of your rental car."

"Only one, my sweet. And you'd be surprised what a gentleman of my experience can do with one hand."

"I'm not a bit worried. I plan to sit as far away from you as possible."

"You'll change your mind, my dear."

They stepped out into the night. The City of Light was alive before them, a sprawling giant wearing a patchwork coat of light and shadow, a restless Amazon announcing its presence with raucous laughter and beeping horns and rumbling trains and staccato footsteps upon the pavement. Against the backdrop, Samuel took Molly into his arms.

The move was unexpected. She wasn't prepared to feel his broad chest, his thighs pressing against hers, his demanding lips. He kissed her. It had been only yesterday and it had been forever.

She melted against him, and it was like coming home. His mouth was sweet, his touch tender. Almost, she fell in love. Almost, she gave up her fight for freedom. Almost, but not quite. A small part of her held back from the compelling danger of a commitment to Samuel Adams.

She was only vaguely aware of people passing by them on the sidewalk. Samuel filled her consciousness. Was he more passionate than she remembered, or was that her own heightened response? She was still reeling from their encounter on the dance floor. She supposed she could excuse her near-hussy behavior on the sidewalk by saying that she was tired and overwhelmed and too darned young to withstand the passionate advances of this handsome, experienced older man.

When he finally let her go, she brushed her hand through her hair and tried to look stern. "My goodness. On the sidewalk, Samuel!"

He roared with laughter. "My sweet, you are a delicious fraud." He took her elbow and helped her into his car.

She forgot all about scooting over to the other side. Samuel smiled but didn't comment. Instead he put one arm around her shoulders and deftly maneuvered the car with the other.

She sighed and moved closer. "I've always loved Paris at night."

"So do I...now."

They didn't speak for a while. The comfortable silence was broken by the swish of tires on the street and

the occasional honking of an irate taxi driver. Molly stifled a yawn with the back of her hand.

"Sleepy, my love?" He gently urged her closer.

She put her head on his shoulder. It felt so comfortable, she decided there would be no harm in resting a
while longer. Her eyelids drooped. And then she was
sound asleep.

Samuel smiled down at her. "Sleep, my beautiful Venus. You're going to need it." He chuckled softly to
himself.

He drove with one hand, cuddling Molly close with
the other. He missed her apartment building the first
time he drove by, and had to circle the block, but he
didn't mind. As long as he was holding Molly in his
arms, he was content.

He parked at the curb and smiled down at her. Even
in sleep she had that determined expression that so de-
lighted him.

He bent over and kissed her cheek. "Wake up, my
love. We're home."

"Hmm." She woke slowly, stretching in an unconsciously provocative way that drove Samuel wild.

"Don't do that, Molly."

"What?" She turned her innocent, sleep-refreshed
face to him.

He tenderly brushed her hair back from her forehead. "Never mind, love." He helped her from the car
and up the steps to her apartment.

She didn't come fully awake until she was standing in
front of the elevator. It was an old-fashioned security
cage with a French door and a sliding metal grate.

"Where's the key, my sweet?"

She blushed. "Don't look." Turning her back quickly,
she fished inside her bra and pulled out a tiny coin purse

that held her keys and enough change for a phone call and a taxi.

Samuel chuckled. "Anything in there for me?"

"Certainly not, you brazen pirate."

He steadied her hand with his and opened the French door. Behind it, the elevator grate slid open. Molly stepped inside and leaned against the sides of the metal cage. Samuel placed his hands around her shoulders and moved in close.

"If I were a pirate, my love, I would simply throw you over my shoulder and take you captive."

"You've already done that. Remember?"

"Only the first part." His eyes darkened. "I was foolish not to do the second part, as well."

His lips brushed across her cheek and down the side of her throat. Her body went liquid.

"I love you, Molly." His open mouth traced the elegant line of her shoulder and then dipped lower to skim across the tops of her breasts. She made a small sound of pleasure, and her skin seemed to tighten. Her quick response pleased him.

With one hand he pulled her hips against his. Their harsh breathing combined with the creaking of cables as the ancient elevator rose to the top of the eighteenth-century apartment building.

"How will I ever tame the beast long enough to court you properly?" he murmured against the side of her throat.

She didn't care about being courted properly...or any other way. Samuel was doing a pretty darned good job of sweeping her off her feet. At that moment if he had said *Let's get married right here in this elevator*, she wouldn't have had the will or the strength to do otherwise.

The elevator creaked to a stop.

"This is my floor, Samuel."

"Which apartment number?"

"Sixty."

He picked her up and carried her to her door. Naked bulbs in the dimly lit hall shone down on her hair.

"You look like an angel, my sweet."

"I'm not."

"I'm glad." He kissed her cheek and set her on her feet. "Where's your key?"

"You can't come in."

"Molly, I have no intention of coming inside. That would be too much temptation for any man to bear... Are you going to get the key, or shall I?" He lifted one eyebrow.

She whirled quickly and retrieved her key from its nesting place. It fit into the lock on the third try. She started to turn the doorknob, but Samuel stayed her hand.

"I'll see you in the morning, love. Ten o'clock."

"How do you know I'll be here? I'm a working girl."

"Surely not on Saturday?" Her face told him he'd guessed right. He turned, opened her apartment door, and let her in. "See you tomorrow, Venus."

One final kiss on the cheek, and he was gone. Molly stood in the dark and wondered what she would do now.

"Do you want to turn on the light? Or shall we talk in the dark?"

She jumped at the sound. Robin rose from the sofa and flicked on a lamp. Taking Molly's hand he led her back to the couch.

"I guessed you'd want to talk."

Molly sank onto the cushions and put her head on her friend's shoulder. He patted her arm.

"What in the world am I going to do, Robin?"

"I'm not one to advise, *chérie*, but I can listen."

Molly sighed and stared into space for a while, and then she began to talk. "He says he loves me...and I think that's true. He wants to marry me."

"How do you feel, *chérie*?"

"Scared. Uncertain."

"That's not like my Molly."

"I know. But then, I've never been this close to falling in love."

"You love him?"

"I don't know."

"Why don't you find out?"

"How?"

"I'm sure you'll think of something."

They sat on the sofa without talking, best of friends, content to enjoy each other's company. Molly almost dropped off to sleep. And in that moment of perfect clarity between waking and sleeping, a plan came to her.

She sat up and looked at Robin. "Why didn't I think of that sooner?"

"Judging by that radiant smile on your face, you've come up with a plan. It must be good...and very naughty. Tell me."

"I'm almost afraid to say it out loud. Lean close."

He did, and she whispered in his ear.

"Of course. It's the French way."

"No, it's not merely that. Don't you see? I can find out if all these..." She made a gesture of frustration with her hands.

"Passions?"

"Yes. Without making any commitments, I can see if it's love or just lust. I'll still be free. And at the same time, I can find out Samuel's true feelings."

"No man in his right mind is going to turn down such an offer."

She smiled. "You don't know Samuel. When I first met him, he thought I was the most scandalous, unsuitable woman he'd ever seen. He says he's over that, but I'm not sure." Her smile grew bigger. "Tomorrow I'll find out."

"I suppose I shall have to resign myself to sitting here alone all weekend. I won't even know how things come out until you get back."

She chuckled at Robin's deadpan expression. Leaning over, she pinched his cheeks.

"You're a great pal."

"So are you, *chérie*." He stood up and took her hand. "Bedtime. You have to look your best for tomorrow."

The persistent sound woke Samuel. Groggily he reached for his alarm clock. When his hand came up empty, he realized that he wasn't in Florence, Alabama; he was in Paris. And the noise wasn't an alarm clock— it was someone knocking on his door. He fumbled in the dark for his watch. The glowing dial said eight o'clock.

"Dammit," he muttered as he reached for his pants. "Don't the French maids sleep?"

There was more tapping at his door, louder this time.

"Coming!" he called. He reached for his shirt and then discarded it. If the French maids insisted on barging into his room at this hour, they could very well take what they found.

His bare feet sank into the plush carpet as he made his way to the door. Latches and chains rattled, and he swung the door open.

Molly was standing in the hallway, dressed in a pert red suit and a sassy hat with a small veil.

"Good Lord! Molly!"

"Is that the same as 'Good morning, Molly'?" He stared at her and she grinned. "Are you going to invite me in or shall we stand all day in the hallway?" She reached out and boldly ran her hands down his bare chest. "We might create a sensation."

He stepped back from the door. "Come in."

"Can you help me with these bags?"

"What bags?"

For the first time since he'd opened the door, he looked at something besides Molly's smiling face and stunning figure. She was surrounded by bags, all of them red—hatboxes and hanging bags and suitcases and cosmetic cases—enough to outfit a regiment of French soldiers.

She smiled sweetly. He didn't trust that smile for a minute. "I paid the bellboy a handsome sum to bring the bags up and then to leave without putting them into the room." She lifted a red hatbox. "Do you mind?"

He was wide-awake now, his mind spinning with possibilities. Molly on his doorstep with her bags... She was up to devilment.

He took the hatbox and her arm at the same time. "Do come in. Make yourself comfortable."

She marched into his hotel room like a queen making her entrance to hold court. He started whistling and bringing in bags, all the while watching her out of the corner of his eye.

First she opened the draperies to let in the light. Next she turned on three lamps. With her hands propped on her sassy hips, she surveyed the room. When she looked at the bed, she blushed and looked away quickly.

Samuel stifled a chuckle that threatened to ruin his whistling.

With all her bags inside, piled neatly in a corner of his room, he pulled out a chair. "Sit down, my sweet." She obeyed. He noticed that she seemed less sure of herself now. He was glad. Her innocence was one of the most appealing things about her. "To what do I owe the pleasure of this visit?"

"This is not a visit."

He cocked one expressive eyebrow at her. "It's not?"

"No. I'm moving in."

He held back his grin. "Don't you think the room is a little small for two?"

"It will do."

"There's only one bed."

"We'll share."

"What did you say, my love? I didn't quite catch that."

"We'll both sleep in the same bed."

He had to force himself to sit calmly in his chair. Every fiber in him strained to stalk across the room, throw Molly over his shoulder and take her to that bed she was so insistent on sharing. "Is this a proposal, Molly? If so, I accept."

"No. This is not a proposal." She got up and began to pace the room. Her little hat slipped down over one eye and threatened to tumble off her head. She paced and paced, biting her lip and working up her courage. This wasn't as easy as she had thought it would be. And then there was Samuel. She hadn't known what his reaction would be. But then, Samuel always did the unexpected. She'd have to be careful, she decided. That's all.

Finally she stopped her pacing, clasped her hands in front of her, and turned to face him.

"I'm moving in with you . . . as your lover."

"You want to have an affair?"

"Yes."

He sat so still that he might suddenly have turned to bronze. Molly watched him. His face told her nothing, but his body was tense. Was he going to turn her down? she wondered. After all her planning, was he going to say *no*?

He stood and slowly walked toward her. She made herself wait for him. After all, she was the one who had said she wanted an affair.

"I suppose you're willing to start right away?" He came closer and closer. She could see a muscle jumping in his jaw and a flame deep in the center of his black eyes.

"Of course."

He had reached her now. The sun's morning rays streaked his chest and tipped his dark chest hair with gold. In order to avoid looking into his face, she focused on his chest.

She felt her hat being lifted off. There was a quick flick of Samuel's wrist. The hat went flying across the room and landed on the bed. Still, she couldn't bring herself to lift her gaze from his chest.

Without a word, he unfastened the top button of her suit. She could feel the heat of his hands all the way through her clothes. He popped the second button open, and the third. She could scarcely breathe.

"Changed your mind, my sweet?"

"No."

"Good." He slid her jacket from her shoulders. Underneath, her silky blouse clung to her damp skin.

"It's awfully hot in here, don't you think?"

He almost smiled. "You need some air?"

"Please."

"I could open a window."

"That would be fine." He stood for a moment, gazing down at her. When he finally spoke, his voice was soft and tender. "Or we could go out for some air."

Reprieve, she thought. She gave him a brilliant smile. "What a great idea. I love Paris in the summer, and it's a beautiful morning."

He smiled. "Why don't you change into something suitable for walking while I shower?"

He whistled all the way to the bathroom. The minute the door closed behind him, she quickly opened a suitcase and pulled out shorts, a blouse and walking shoes. Her hands fumbled on the buttons of her blouse as she started undressing.

"Darn!" She bit her lip hard enough to cause pain. She had to pull herself together. It wouldn't do for Samuel to know that she was new at this game. Her success depended on scandalizing him so that he would head back to America. That way, nobody would be hurt. She wouldn't have to turn down his proposal; and she wouldn't have to risk loving and losing. What if she did have to lose her virginity? Under the circumstances, it was all she could think to do. Anyhow, she supposed that was a fair exchange for freedom.

She quickly finished dressing and was just tying her shoes when Samuel came out of the bathroom, still whistling. She looked up, half expecting to see him wearing nothing more than a towel, but he surprised her. He was fully dressed, wearing snug-fitting jeans and a white T-shirt. He looked virile and handsome and altogether delicious.

She decided the affair wasn't such a bad idea, after all. There were many women who would even envy her.

"There's a wonderful park at the Champ de Mars," she said. "There are carousels and puppet shows and donkey rides. We could spend the entire day at the park."

"I haven't see a puppet show since I was ten...."

A large chunk of her heart became his forever. If she kept losing pieces of her heart to him, soon he would have it all.

She became brisk and businesslike. "We can pick up sandwiches at the corner deli and pack a picnic lunch."

"Whatever happened to breakfast?"

"We'll start with croissants and *café au lait*."

"All your ideas are wonderful, Molly."

She shot a quick glance at his face, but all she saw was a friendly smile.

"Shall we go, my dear?" He took her hand and led her out the door.

Chapter Nine

By the time they reached the park, it was almost noon. The Eiffel Tower presided over brightly colored gardens of summer flowers and quiet tree-shaded walks. The music of the carousels blended with the happy laughter of children.

Samuel and Molly strolled through the crowd.

"Look, Samuel . . . a puppet show."

A gaily striped awning shaded a small stage. Marionettes danced and sang, their wooden legs tapping against the stage floor.

Molly tugged his hand, urging him forward. The puppeteers were singing in French, and Samuel didn't understand a word they said. What he did understand was the enchantment on Molly's face. Her eyes were alight with childlike wonder and her face shone with innocent joy.

In his hard-nosed business world, he rarely saw such a face. Even his social world was woefully lacking in joyful people. Watching her, he understood why he had fallen so unexpectedly in love. From the very beginning, her gay spirit had been a balm to his scarred and tattered soul. Each time he had tried to deny his feelings, he had felt as if he were leaving the sunshine and plunging into a cold, dark abyss.

He wished he knew the perfect words to say to her, the perfect things to do for her. But he was only human; he'd have to content himself with muddling through. And he could only hope that that would be enough. His hand tightened on hers. If he lost Molly, he might as well buy a one-way ticket to hell, for he knew that life without her would be unbearable.

He leaned down and planted a tender kiss on the top of her head.

She gazed up at him. "Wasn't that show wonderful?"

"Is it over?"

"Weren't you watching the show?"

"I was watching you."

"Then you missed all the fun."

"On the contrary. Molly-watching is my favorite pastime." Her blush made him smile. "Anyhow, I don't understand French."

"Then we'll have to find some other entertainment for you."

"I can think of about a thousand entertainments . . . and all of them involving you." He set the picnic basket on the ground and pulled her into his arms. With one finger, he tipped her face up to his. "I haven't kissed you this morning, Molly. It's time to remedy that."

It was a lover's kiss—thorough and very tender. Carousel music echoed across the park, and the sweet fragrance of summer flowers filled the air. And Molly knew. Suddenly she knew beyond a shadow of a doubt that she was in love with Samuel Adams. True, she had been feeling passion...and desire. He had awakened yearnings in her body that she had never known existed. But what she felt now went beyond passion, beyond desire. She felt an intense need to wrap this man around her heart and hold him there forever.

She eased her hands around his neck and pulled him closer. Standing on tiptoe, she fitted herself more perfectly against his body.

Samuel sensed the change in her. He deepened the kiss, parting her lips and plunging his tongue into the warm honey of her mouth.

The Champ de Mars was designed for lovers. Throngs of laughing children and indulgent adults passed them without a glance. The carousel continued its mechanical musical rounds and the puppeteers geared up for another show.

Still, Samuel kissed his Molly. It was a kiss full of joy in the moment and promises for the future.

When he finally released her, Molly leaned her head against his chest. Joy surged through her; and on its heels, fear. If only love came with guarantees. Samuel was with her now, but how did she know he wouldn't be snatched out of her life tomorrow, or the next day, or the next? She couldn't handle it. Not yet. Not now. Maybe not ever.

Lifting her head, she spoke with determined gaiety. "I'm ravenous, Samuel. Let's eat."

"Already? After all those sweet rolls you had for breakfast?" He grasped the picnic basket and led her toward a grove of trees. "I'll have to sell stock in order to raise the funds to feed you." His laughter was light-hearted.

"Don't . . ."

When he saw her face, the laughter stopped. "What's wrong?"

For a moment, she thought of confiding in him. But the moment passed quickly.

"Don't keep lagging behind, Sammy boy. A young girl like me could starve to death while she waits for an old man to catch up."

She grabbed the picnic basket and ran ahead of him.

"I'll get you for that, Venus."

He strolled along, content to watch Molly as she raced toward the trees. Those legs! he thought. A man could be content just looking at those legs for the rest of his life.

By the time he reached her, she had already spread out their lunch and was busy stuffing ham and cheese into huge hunks of French bread. He sat down beside her and uncorked the wine.

Her gaiety continued throughout the lunch and for the rest of the afternoon. While they were riding the carousel, Samuel became aware that Molly's high spirits were forced. What had happened? he wondered. When he had kissed her, he'd been certain that she yielded, that she was open to his courtship.

He leaned over and spoke loud enough to be heard above the sound of music.

"Is something bothering you, Molly?"

"Certainly not. It's a beautiful day and I'm with my lover. What more could a girl want?"

Her denial was too quick, too pat. "What more, indeed." She was hiding something from him, and he had every intention of finding out what it was.

After the carousel ride, Samuel suggested they go back to his hotel. He deliberately cut short their day in the park, for he had pressing matters to take care of.

It was only four o'clock when they got back to their hotel room. Samuel disappeared into the bathroom, whistling, and left Molly to gaze at the bed. It seemed to have grown bigger in their absence. Love in the afternoon. She supposed that's why Samuel had come back so early.

What was she supposed to do now? Seduce him, she guessed. After all, she was the one who had asked for the affair. She wondered if she was supposed to strip all the way or if she could get by with merely taking off her shoes. Lands, she was so nervous, you'd think she had never been naked in front of a man before. She hadn't, really. Posing nude for artists didn't count.

She took off her shoes and lined them neatly under the bed. She caught sight of herself in the mirror. Her hair was disheveled and she had a smudge of dirt on her cheek. Nobody in his right mind would find that sexy. She ran a comb through her hair and rubbed at the smudge. What was he doing in the bathroom so long? She decided to find out.

She tiptoed to the bathroom door and listened. Water was running. He was *showering*. That sounded serious to her. Maybe she should put on a sexy gown. At four in the afternoon? Who was she kidding?

She glanced at the bed again. Now *there* was an idea. She unbuttoned her blouse and threw it across a chair. Next she shed her bra. Then she tiptoed toward the bed.

"Molly!"

She dived into the bed and pulled the sheet up over her breasts.

Samuel came through the bathroom door. For goodness' sake, she thought. He was dressed in a three-piece suit and tie. And here she was in bed.

He leaned against the doorframe and surveyed the scene before him. Molly's hair was fetchingly tumbled over her bare shoulders, and a hint of dirt was still on her cheeks. She seemed to collect smudges the way some people collect fine art. She was holding on to the sheet as if her life depended on it.

"I see you're already in bed."

Don't panic, she told herself. "Yes. I was feeling a little sleepy."

"Sleepy?"

"Yes. I thought a nap would be nice." She stretched and yawned to make her lie sound authentic. The sheet slid downward. She grabbed for it, but she was nervous and Samuel was faster.

In three strides he was across the room, leaning over the bed and holding the runaway sheet in one hand.

"Did you drop something?"

She figured a real-live mistress would know what to do when a man looked at your naked breasts that way, but all she could do was sit there tongue-tied. It was embarrassing.

"Not deliberately." His eyes crinkled at the corners. She hastily amended her quick confession. "I mean . . . don't you think it's a little chilly in here?"

"It must be. You have chill bumps." He pulled the sheet over her shoulders and patted her on the head. "Why don't you take that nap now, my dear? You're going to need your rest for tonight."

She thought she heard him chuckling as he walked toward the door but she couldn't be sure. It was hard to tell over the rumbling of her stomach. It always growled when she was nervous.

The door clicked shut behind Samuel. Molly threw the sheet aside and stormed out of bed.

"Good grief!" She paced the floor, punching the air with her fists. "Hell's bells!"

She stomped around the room for ten minutes before she began to calm down. Then she picked up the phone and dialed her apartment.

Robin answered on the fourth ring.

"What took you so long?"

"Molly, is that you?"

"Yes, it's me."

"I didn't expect to hear from you, at least not for a few days."

"I didn't expect to be talking to you, either, but if I don't talk to somebody I'm going to explode."

"Is it that good or that bad?"

"Good grief, I don't know. We spent all day at the park, and then suddenly he decided to come back to the hotel. Naturally, I assumed . . . that is, I thought . . ."

"That he wanted to make love?"

"Right. Anyway, he went to the bathroom and I decided to undress and wait for him in bed. Well, I didn't actually undress . . . not all of me. I decided to take off my top so it would look like I was undressed. I figured if he got serious, he could handle my shorts. And then, of course—"

"Molly."

"What!"

"Calm down, *chérie*."

"What am I doing wrong, Robin?"

"It's not you, Molly. It's him. I've heard American men are very uncreative about sex. Perhaps he's the kind who has to wait until he's watched the ten o'clock nightly news.''

"Lands, I hope not!"

Robin laughed. "Maybe you can change his mind, *chérie*."

"How?"

"Well, I'm no expert, but here's what I think you should do..."

Samuel was late. He had intended to be back at the hotel by eight o'clock, but it was already nine and he guessed Molly must be starving. Perhaps she had ordered dinner sent up or had gone downstairs to a restaurant. He hoped so.

He set all his packages on the floor so he could get to the key in his pocket. He'd been quite successful with his errands, but his phone calls to America hadn't paid off. Jedidiah and Glory Ethel didn't answer. He had wanted to know everything about Molly—her childhood, her schools, her teachers, her hobbies, her friends—anything that would give him a clue to her behavior. Jedidiah could have told him those things. He had to know why she was so determined to get him out of her life.

He swung the door open. Gossamer curtains billowed against his face, candles glowed on every available surface, and the heady fragrance of perfume almost made him dizzy. His entire hotel room was hung with gauzy curtains and strewn with satin pillows—*scarlet* satin. From somewhere in that maze of Arabian Nights paraphernalia he heard soft music and the electric whirring of fans. That's why the curtains were blowing against his face.

"Molly?" The candlelight made it hard to see. "Molly?" He parted the curtains and stopped short.

Molly was in the center of the room reclining on a pile of scarlet cushions. He didn't know what to call that outfit she was wearing, if it could even be called an outfit. He doubted it. There wasn't enough cloth to make a decent-size handkerchief. And what little there was was so thin he could see right through it.

Forgetting his packages in the hall, he moved closer. The door clicked shut behind him.

Molly smiled. He guessed you could call it a smile. It looked like pure seduction to him. Every fiber of his body stood up and saluted.

"I see you've been busy this afternoon."

She didn't say a word. With one hand she tossed her long golden hair over her shoulder and lazily patted the cushions beside her.

"Why don't you join me, lover?"

He sat down. *Sank* would be a more appropriate term, he thought, for his legs could no longer support him. The cushions were soft and Molly was sweet and her fragrance was intoxicating. He did what any red-blooded male would do: he wrapped his arms around her and lowered her to the cushions.

She stiffened, but only briefly. The minute his lips touched hers, she was his. He knew that. No man of his experience could fail to recognize the yielding of a passionate woman. Kissing her with unbridled desire, he did what was only natural for a man in his condition: he fitted himself expertly into every soft curve and hollow of her perfect body. Sensations rocked him. Never had he felt naked in a three-piece business suit—never until this moment.

Her hips moved. Whether it was unconscious or deliberate, he didn't know; and he was past caring. He ran his hands down the length of her legs. Molly's response heated his blood.

Lifting himself on his elbows, he pushed aside the wisp of fabric that covered her breasts. Candlelight flickered over her creamy skin. With one finger, he traced the pattern of light. Molly sucked in her breath.

It was that one small sound that brought him to his senses. Not like this, he thought. He wouldn't take Molly like this.

He pulled the fabric back over her breasts. Somebody somewhere ought to give him a medal. He figured that he was a hero worthy of decoration.

"Samuel?"

He smiled down at her. "Not that you don't tempt me, Molly. On the contrary, I've never been more tempted in my life."

"But I thought affairs..."

He hushed her with one finger over her lips. "We won't be having an affair, Molly." He smiled at the look of relief that flooded her face. Slipping an arm under her shoulders, he lifted her off the cushions. Keeping one arm around her, he pulled her close. "You see, Molly, I'm in love with you. I won't allow you to be a weekend lover for any man, not even myself." She leaned against his chest, listening. He smoothed her hair as he talked. "I don't understand why you're doing this, but that doesn't matter...."

"I thought you would be so disgusted and scandalized that you'd leave and go back to America."

"Is that what you want me to do?"

"I... don't think so. Not anymore."

"I'm glad, Molly." He kissed the top of her head, then stood. "Do you mind if I blow out a few of these candles? I'm afraid the room is going to catch on fire."

"By my guest."

He blew out the candles nearest the door. While he was up, he switched off the electric fan. The floating curtains settled down. Behind him, Molly rose from the cushions and flicked on a lamp.

"I never thought this would work anyhow," she muttered.

"It worked all right, my dear. Almost too well." He crossed the room and took her by the shoulders. "You brought out more than the beast in me tonight, Molly. You came very close to being ravished." He urged her into his arms and began to caress her back. "I'd like a repeat performance in...say, six or seven weeks...after we've been married awhile and I'm beginning to lose interest."

Her chin came up and her eyes blazed. "If I can't hold your interest longer than that, my name's not Venus de Molly."

It was the first time she'd ever failed to protest marriage. He was elated.

"Well, perhaps you could save this Arabian Nights fantasy awhile...until I'm a hundred and ten and you're..."

"You're crazy." Her laughter was bright and happy.

"I'm crazy in love." He kissed her soundly to prove his point. After it was over, he had to take off his jacket and loosen his tie to release the heat. He tossed them carelessly across a chair—a first for him—and started toward the door. "Wait right here, Molly."

"There aren't many places I can go dressed like this."

She waited in the curtain-hung bedroom while he retrieved boxes and bags from the hallway.

"It looks like Christmas," she said.

"It feels like Christmas." He heaved the last of the boxes inside and shut the door. "Fortune has smiled on us, Molly. All the packages were still there, even the ice cream."

"The ice cream?"

"Yes. And the cherries and the whipped cream and the chocolate syrup and the popcorn drizzled with butter." He unloaded the boxes and bags as he talked.

As she watched, every item she had mentioned in that backyard on Church Street came to light—a circus poster and two tickets to the circus; three carousel music boxes, all playing different tunes; a windup teddy bear dressed in marching-band uniform and beating a tiny tin drum; tickets to the Comédie-Française and the Opéra.

One of the packages barked.

"Samuel? Is that a dog?"

"Poor little beggar." Samuel lifted the cover off the dog carrier and a small white furry face peered through the bars. The puppy barked again.

Molly knelt beside the carrier and lifted the miniature poodle out. She cuddled her face to his soft fur.

"A puppy! I can't believe you bought a puppy."

Samuel knelt beside her and lavished his attention on both of them, alternately rubbing the puppy's coat and Molly's back. Eventually, though, Molly was receiving the lion's share of petting.

"I love dogs, Molly, and circuses and theater and chocolate sundaes and buttered popcorn. It wasn't until I met you that I realized I could make time for those small pleasures." He sat on the floor and pulled her into his arms, puppy and all. "I love children, too, but you can't just go out on the street and buy them."

She chuckled. "I guess we'll have to settle for the old-fashioned way."

"Molly...is that a yes to the proposal I'm getting around to?"

She leaned her head against his chest. The steady throb of his heart under her cheek reassured her. Samuel was well and healthy...alive. Nothing could ever happen to him.

She lifted her head to look into his face. It was dearer to her than any face she'd ever known...dearer than Papa's, even. What if...

"Molly?"

She simply wasn't going to think about it any longer. She was going to seize the day.

"Yes, Samuel. Oh, yes." She kissed him and might have gone on kissing him until morning if the puppy hadn't protested.

Laughing together, they sat on the scarlet cushions and ate the cold popcorn and the melting sundaes while the music boxes played and the puppy cavorted among the gossamer curtains. Then they lay back on the pillows. Between kisses they described to each other the exact moment they had fallen in love.

"I think it was when I saw your gold-snake sandals," Samuel said.

"It took me a while longer. You were standing under that painting of mine in Papa's house, talking about having once loved someone who broke the rules."

"Let's break a few rules, Molly. Let's get married here, in Paris."

"You don't want a traditional wedding with our parents and friends?"

"We can have one of those, too, if you like, when we get back to the States."

"Samuel, I'm willing to break all the rules for you."

* * *

It was after midnight when he carried her back to her apartment—puppy, bags and all.

After Samuel had gone, Robin came out of his bedroom, rubbing the sleep from his eyes. "Molly? *Mon dieu!* What happened?"

"Things didn't work out the way I had planned."

"That's terrible."

"No, it's wonderful." The puppy barked his agreement.

"What is that creature in your arms?"

"My wedding gift from Samuel. His name is Pirate."

He sat on the sofa and rubbed his eyes again. "I guess I had too many beers. Or maybe I've just missed something. You did say *wedding*, didn't you?"

"I did, and you're going to be the best man."

"Whatever happened to falling in love first?"

"I already did that, Robin. It just took me a long time to realize it." She sat beside him on the sofa. "If you have an hour or two, I'll tell you exactly how I fell in love with Samuel and why I was too stubborn to admit it."

"Wait right there, Molly. I'll heat the coffee."

Samuel and Molly were married in the park, with Robin and Pirate and six of Molly's artist friends as witnesses. Although the planning time had been exceedingly short, Robin insisted on a wedding cake, which he baked. It was his favorite kind: banana-raisin with plenty of nuts.

Molly and Samuel sneaked away while their seven guests as well as assorted birds and a few gray squirrels were enjoying the wedding cake. Samuel tried not to break the speed limit getting back to the hotel in his rental car. He made it, just barely.

He whisked Molly and Pirate into the elevator and down the hallway to his room. He carried both Molly and her dog over the threshold.

"Mrs. Adams, have I told you today that I love you?"

"Only sixteen times. I'm feeling a little deprived."

"I'll have to think of some way to make it up to you." He took the little dog from her arms and transferred him to the doggie basket in the bathroom. "Sorry, little fellow. You'll have to play with your plastic mouse for a while. I have plans for your mistress."

When Samuel came back to Molly, her cheeks were glowing. He caught her face between his hands.

"Molly, I've waited forever for you."

"And I, for you."

His hands dropped to her shoulders. "I promise that I will never make you sorry you married me."

"You don't have to promise that, Samuel. I know it."

"It's important to me that you know you can trust me."

"I do."

He held her close, caressing the length of her back until the rhythm of her heart became steady.

"Molly, I want to make love to you, my sweet."

"Yes." Her voice was muffled against his chest.

"I'll be gentle."

"Samuel..." She lifted her head, her eyes bright. "I want everything—thundering heart and sweaty limbs and a wild ride into paradise."

He threw back his head and laughed. "Venus, what books have you been reading lately?"

"None. That's how Robin described it to me."

"It wouldn't do to make Robin a liar, now would it?" His hands caught the zipper at the back of her dress and slowly pulled it downward. He put his hands on her shoulders and began to slide the dress off. She put her hands over him.

"Let me." She took his hand and led him to a chair beside the bed, and then she stepped back. The curtains were drawn against the afternoon sun. A small lamp provided the only light in the room.

Samuel watched as Molly walked toward the radio. Where her zipper gaped open, he could see a gleaming strip of skin. That one small patch of skin was more exciting than an entire lineup of gorgeous Las Vegas women.

Molly fiddled with the radio until she found a station that played mood music. The soft sound of blues filled the room. She turned slowly, using her body the way a violinist uses a fine Stradivarius. With languid movements, she removed her dress. It slithered down her body, inch by enticing inch. She was wearing black satin underneath her dress. Tiny black straps barely marked her creamy shoulders. Black satin dipped low over her breasts and lightly skimmed her hips. The satin was cropped short and slit high, showcasing her here-to-eternity legs.

The dress pooled at her feet. She stepped out of it and moved it aside with a delicate flick of her foot. Her shoes were strappy little black leather sandals with heels at least four inches high.

Samuel's mouth went dry. "What is that garment you're wearing?"

"It's called a chemise." She ran her hands down her body with agonizing slowness. "Do you like it?"

"I'm going to see that you have three million of those things, for I plan to rip one off you every day for the rest of our lives."

She stretched like a lazy cat, lifting one shoulder higher than the other so that one tiny black strap slid downward. "Be my guest, Samuel."

He was across the room in three strides. Their gazes locked as he caught the front of her chemise.

"You're sure, my love?"

"I want to be wild and wanton for you, Samuel."

The sound of tearing fabric blended with the wail of blues music. Samuel's breath caught as the black satin parted. Molly was braless. He couldn't take his eyes off her.

The torn chemise slid to the floor as he reached out to cup her breasts.

"I knew you were beautiful, Molly, but I had no idea..." His hands explored, sending shivers through her body. She felt herself tightening, aching, for him.

"Molly." He lowered his mouth to her right breast.

She tangled her hands in his hair. "Paradise," she whispered. "You've already shown me paradise."

"Not yet, my sweet. We've only just begun."

He moved his hands down, tracing the lines of her body, leaving a trail of shivers in the wake. His thumbs hooked in the minuscule black lace G-string and stripped it aside. Then he lifted Molly and carried her to the bed.

Her hair fanned out against the covers in a lustrous mass of silky gold. "I could spend the rest of my life merely looking at you."

She reached for him and he obliged by bending over her. She raked her fingers along his bare back.

"How can I get a thundering heart if all you do is look?"

His chuckle was deep and satisfied. "I married a wanton...thank God." He made quick work of his pants.

Lying on the bed facing her, her took one of her hands in his. "Touch me, Molly." He guided her hand across his chest. "Does that feel good to you?"

"Yes."

He moved her hand lower. "And that?"

"Oh, yes."

He squeezed her hand and she gasped with pleasure.

"I never knew, Samuel."

"I'm glad...so very glad." He skimmed his hands over her, memorizing her perfect body, cataloging forever the satin texture of her skin.

Heat raced through her. His sensuous exploration aroused her in ways she'd never known possible. She began to writhe under his touch, tossing restlessly against the covers.

"Please...Oh, Samuel..."

He lifted himself over her and made her his own. With her warmth surrounding him, he gazed into her face. "I love you, Molly...I love you...."

His whispers trailed off as he took Molly to a place she'd never been, high above the stars, soaring through a galaxy exploding with heat and light.

Chapter Ten

The next three days were perfect for the newlyweds. In the daytime they explored Paris and at night they explored each other. The tickets to the Opéra and the Comédie-Française sat on the dresser, unused.

On the fourth day, Samuel began to talk of going home. He leaned over Molly in the bed and watched the play of morning sunlight on her naked thigh.

Propped high against the pillows, feeling contented and much loved, Molly smiled at him.

"See anything you like?"

He kissed a spot, warm from the sunshine. "If you have a year or two, I'll tell you exactly what I like."

"You can have the next hundred years. I'll be here at your side."

"Here in Paris, Molly?"

"Wherever you are, Samuel."

"We never talked much about the future. It's time we should."

"I guess we got carried away." She laced her hands around his neck and pulled him down to the pillows.

Nuzzling her face against his throat, she murmured, "It's easy to get carried away with you." Dipping her head lower, she traced a path on his skin with her tongue.

"Molly...if we're going to talk...Molly! My God... we can talk...later."

They never did get around to their talk. After a long, rowdy session in bed, Samuel spent an hour on the phone, checking on his bank, and then he left on business errands.

Molly spent the rest of the morning soaking in the tub and playing with Pirate and anticipating Samuel's return.

"Pirate, I don't know why I didn't try married life sooner. It's wonderful."

He thought she was telling him how wonderful he was, and responded by running in circles and barking with puppy-dog happiness.

At noon Molly ordered lunch sent up, and she was just settling down with her salad when the phone rang. It was Glory Ethel.

"How are you, darling?"

"Wonderful. Marvelous." Molly laughed. "It would cost you a fortune if I told you."

"Is Samuel there?"

"I'm sorry, but you missed him. He called his bank this morning and he's gone off now on some business or other."

"Oh, dear."

"Glory Ethel...is something wrong?"

"Don't get alarmed, dear."

She was. Shivers of premonition began to crawl up her spine.

"Glory Ethel, where's Papa?" There was silence on the other end of the line. "Is Papa there?" She was standing now, her voice high with terror. "Has something happened to Papa?"

"I wanted Samuel to be there when I told you.... I know how you feel about Jedidiah...." Glory choked back a sob.

"Not Papa. Dear God, not Papa!"

Molly's hysterics calmed down Glory Ethel. "It's all right, darling. It's not serious. Jedidiah is okay."

Gradually Glory Ethel's reassurances began to sink in. Molly sat down, her legs weak.

"What happened?"

"I'm just a silly old fool for crying and upsetting you like that. I'm used to having him around...and I miss him so much...and I feel partly responsible. I should have kept him from doing it."

"Doing what? What's wrong with Papa?"

"He has a broken leg, that's all. Not the hip, thank God."

"How did it happen?"

"You know how stubborn your father can be sometimes.... Well, he insisted on mowing the yard himself. He climbed on that cantankerous old riding mower of mine—Land sakes, he doesn't know as much about that machine as I do—anyway, it got away from him and he sideswiped a tree. Broke his right leg below the knee."

"Where is he now?"

"Still in the hospital. They set the leg and put it in a cast, but they decided to keep him for a day or two, just to make sure he didn't do any other damage."

"You're sure he's all right, Glory Ethel? You aren't sugarcoating this, are you?"

"I promise you, Molly, that the only thing wrong with your father now is that the doctors are keeping him at the hospital when he wants to come home. He told them they've put a crimp in his love life."

Molly's laugh was shaky but relieved. She got the number of the hospital from Glory Ethel, and after they had finished their conversation, she called to talk to her papa. Only when she heard the story from his lips was she satisfied that she wasn't going to lose her father.

She was still shaking when she hung up. Her face felt flushed, her heart was beating fast, and she had to lie down on the bed to keep from fainting. Pirate circled the bed, barking.

She thought of Papa, only a foot away from death. If he had run the mower straight into the tree instead of sideways, he would have been killed. Moaning, she covered her face with her hands. Her wedding rings felt cold against her skin.

She pulled her hands back and looked at them. My God, what had she done? What if that had been Samuel? Where was he now? What if some drunken driver ran over him? What if some drug-crazed addict came into the bank where he was and started shooting?

She couldn't stand it. That was all.

Her hands shook as she picked up the phone and called Robin. When he answered, she didn't even bother to say hello.

"I need a favor, Robin."

"Anything, *chérie.*"

She told him what she wanted and why.

"Anything but that. That's not wise. It's impulsive. It's crazy. Molly, don't do this thing."

"I must."

"Where is Samuel?"

"I don't know. Doing business errands, he said."

"Talk to your husband, *chérie*. Just talk to him."

"He would never agree to let me go. This way, it will be his idea and he won't be hurt. I don't want to hurt him."

"He will be devastated. You will be heartbroken."

"Robin, please. I need you."

"You know I'd give you the moon if I could, but I won't do this for you."

"Then will you vacate the apartment for the afternoon so I can get somebody else? Please..."

"Only for this afternoon. But I must tell you that if I can find Samuel, I'm going to warn him about what you're up to."

"I think it will still work."

She pressed her finger over the disconnect button, and then she called her agent.

Robin was agitated when he left the apartment. He loved Molly and hated refusing her anything, but he knew that her latest scheme was mad. She was frightened, that's all. His first thought was to go to her at the hotel and offer his comfort. Perhaps he could still talk her out of her plan. But what if he missed her? What if she had already left to find some other willing artist? Then he would have wasted valuable time. Instead, he concentrated on trying to locate Samuel.

He'd start with the banks.

Samuel was not at any of the bank locations. He had visited two that morning, and now he was strolling down the street to a corner vendor. He wanted to buy some flowers for Molly.

The flower cart was sitting in front of a small art gallery. Samuel looked into the window and all the breath seemed to leave his body. Molly smiled down at him from a huge oil canvas. She was standing waist-deep in water. Droplets of moisture clung to her eyelashes and sparkled on her cheeks and gleamed on her naked breasts.

While he gazed at the painting, two American tourists stopped on the street beside him.

"She's a honey, ain't she, Gert?" The man's accent was broad. Midwestern, Samuel guessed.

"Shameful, that's what I call it, Grover," the woman named Gert said.

Samuel didn't dare look at the speakers. He was having a hard enough time as it was.

"Hell, Gert, if you had knockers like that . . ."

Samuel didn't wait to hear more. He stalked into the gallery and pointed to the painting in the window. "I'll take that one."

The gallery owner smiled at him. "Sir, I'll be with you in a moment, please."

Now that he was out of earshot of the obnoxious man admiring his wife's body, Samuel began to calm down. He noticed that there were several customers in the store, and that they were in the midst of a purchase. He rammed his hands in his pockets and strolled around the gallery.

Four nude sketches of Molly graced one wall. A large nude watercolor hung on another. On a stand in the center of the gallery was a small statue, a copy of Venus de Molly, his wife, sculpted in bronze.

Samuel hadn't bargained on his reaction. The idea that other men would have the pleasure of seeing Molly's nude body, even if it was in the name of art, filled him with awesome rage. Suddenly he realized that he and Molly had never talked about her career—about whether she would give it up, was *willing* to give it up, or whether she would continue to pose as an artist's model. And if.

she did, could he endure it? His wife...taking off her clothes for other men.

He counted the artwork featuring Molly in the gallery—four sketches, one watercolor, one oil and one bronze. He'd buy them all. That would set him back a pretty penny, he'd dare say. It would be impossible to buy every existing work of Molly. He knew that. But he was going to buy all of these. He'd be damned if he was going to let that foulmouthed Grover get his hands on any of them.

"Can I help you, sir?"

Samuel turned toward the owner of the gallery. "I'll take this copy of the Venus de Molly and every work you have that features her."

"All of them, sir?"

"All of them."

"A very wise choice, sir. This model is at the very height of her popularity now. These pieces can only appreciate in value."

Samuel paid for his artwork and ordered them wrapped and sent to his hotel. Two people entered the gallery as he was leaving.

"I fancy that painting in the winder, young feller. How much is it?"

"I'm sorry, sir. It's sold."

Samuel smiled with satisfaction. Thank God, Grover would never get to drool over his wife. He looked at his watch. Four o'clock. He'd been away from Molly far too long. He couldn't wait to hold her, to touch her. But first they had to talk.

He walked to his rental car and started the drive back to his hotel. His hands were tense on the wheel, and he could still hear Grover's comments about his wife.

"Dammit." Rage boiled in his gut and nearly obscured his vision.

Two blocks farther on, he nearly ran a red light. The incident restored his reason. His reaction was bordering on paranoia—the kind that would cripple if not destroy his marriage to Molly. She was his wife, would always be his wife, and he knew Molly well enough to know that she would never be unfaithful to him. What she did was art. Hadn't he learned that lesson already? And hadn't he also learned that he couldn't dictate to her?

He was whistling by the time he got back to his hotel. The key grated in the lock and he pushed open the door.

"Molly?" He had expected her to come running to greet him. She must be sleeping. He walked quietly into the room. The bed was empty. The bathroom door was wide open. She wasn't in there, either.

Suddenly he saw the piece of white paper on the dresser. He crossed the room quickly and picked it up.

Samuel, it read, *I can't stand being away from my work any longer. While these last few days have certainly been amusing*... Amusing! What in the hell had happened while he was gone? He read the rest of the note, his heart thudding with fear. ...*I've missed the fun of posing in the nude.* She'd never called it fun before. *We'll be at my apartment. Come join us.* We!

He crumpled the note and tossed it toward the wastebasket. He missed. It lay on the floor like a large accusing eye, mocking him. Damn. In his eagerness to marry Molly there were many things he'd left undone, unsaid. He'd ignored her career, thinking, he supposed, that it would take care of itself. And he'd never gotten to the bottom of her reasons for evading him for so long. Now he knew why they called love *blind.*

If he wanted to keep Molly and his marriage, he had much catch-up work to do. He turned and left the empty hotel room.

* * *

She had left her apartment door unlocked. Fifteen minutes after he had left his hotel room, Samuel pushed open the door to her apartment.

Molly was there, just as he had expected. She was posing, also as he had expected. What he hadn't counted on was his own quick flash of anger. He lounged against the doorframe, watching, waiting for his initial anger to cool down. This is art, he told himself firmly. Merely art.

She hadn't seen him yet. She was reclining on a fake grass mat, naked except for a strip of cloth that covered her breasts and her hips. In her hands was one ripe, juicy apple. Eve, tempting Adam.

Samuel's glance swung to the artist. He was old—at least sixty-five, maybe more. And he was intent on his work. If he had any prurient interest in Molly, it certainly didn't show.

Samuel must have made some sound, for suddenly Molly saw him. She started to move.

"Please, don't get up." He strode into the room and pulled a straight-backed chair close to the artist's easel. "I'll just sit here so I can enjoy the view."

"I'm posing," Molly said.

"So I see."

She furrowed her brow in astonishment. "I hope you won't start a scene."

"Carry on, my dear. One of us has to work for a living."

"Are you laughing at me, Samuel?" Again she started to rise, and her small covering slipped. She caught at it, and sank back onto the grass mat.

The old artist, who appeared not to have paid any mind to their conversation, said something in French. Samuel didn't have any idea what it was, but Molly went back to her posing.

"I'm not laughing, my sweet. I'm lusting." He tipped his chair back and crossed his hands behind his head. "I hope you'll be finished soon, because I have plans for you."

"I know you hate this, and if you want to talk about divorce..."

"Divorce." He hooted with laughter.

"I knew you'd hate this—seeing me naked with another man—but I didn't think it would make you hysterical."

"I'm not hysterical. I happen to find it all damned funny."

"Funny?"

"My dear, don't you think I see through this latest ploy of yours? You're trying to get rid of me again. And this time, I'm going to find out why."

"Then you're not leaving?"

He let the chair legs back down. They hit the floor with a soft thud. Slowly he stood up and started toward her.

"Molly, I will never leave you. Nor will I ever let you go." His advance was as purposeful as the Americans storming the beach at Normandy. And he had the same thing in mind—victory.

Molly watched him coming. How could she ever have thought she wanted him to leave? she wondered. How could she ever have believed he would?

Never taking her eyes off Samuel's, she spoke in French to the artist. He picked up his paints and canvas and easel and left the apartment. The lock clicked behind him.

Samuel was standing over her now. "It's a good thing you did that, Molly."

"We were finished for the day, anyhow."

In one swift motion, Samuel bent over and lifted her off the mat. Her skimpy covering slid aside.

A flame leaped in the center of his eyes. "We have to talk, Molly."

"Now?"

He smiled. "Later."

He kicked aside the grass-mat prop and lowered Molly to the carpet. Buttons flew in all directions as he ripped his shirt off.

"Better put the night latch on. Robin has a key."

He hurried across the room to do her bidding, shedding his belt and shoes and pants as he went. When he came back, she lifted her arms to him.

He sank onto the carpet and covered his wife. Between fierce kisses, he said, "Don't ever...think... you...can get...rid...of me."

"Never again. Oh, Samuel, do that again."

"That?"

"Ahh, yes." Between gasps of ecstasy, she said, "I was afraid...of losing you. Like I lost my...mother."

With one powerful thrust, Samuel was fully sheathed in her. They didn't talk again for a long, long while. And finally, love sated and sweat slickened, they lay back against the carpet, Samuel's arm around Molly's shoulders and her legs tangled with his.

"When I read your note, I knew something had happened. Can you tell me about it, Molly?"

She smiled. "That's what Robin advised in the first place. He was right."

"Smart fellow, that Robin. I'll have to think of a way to reward him." He lifted her hand and kissed her knuckles, one by one. "We have to trust each other, my love. I know that something has been bothering you for a long time, and I was foolish not to have found out sooner."

"When I lost my mother, I vowed never to let anyone else close enough so that their loss would break my heart. I already had Papa, of course, so he didn't count. Today, when Glory Ethel called to say that Papa had broken his leg, I panicked. He could just as easily have been killed. And I thought, what if it had been you?"

Samuel closed his arms around her and rocked her silently for a moment.

"I can't guarantee that nothing bad will ever happen to me, Molly."

"I know that."

"I wish I could. I want to live forever for you ... and you with me."

"And I with you, Samuel—whatever the risks. I realized that today, the minute you walked through the door."

The night latch rattled. Samuel chuckled. "Speaking of doors..."

"Is that you, Robin?" Molly called.

"It's me."

"Just a minute."

There was a mad scramble for clothes. When they finally let Robin in, he immediately understood the import of what he was seeing. Samuel's shirt was missing its buttons, and Molly had her shorts on inside out.

He grinned. "I don't suppose you two would be interested in a celebration dinner?"

"How did you know?" Molly asked.

"I took a wild guess."

Later that evening Samuel treated Robin to dinner and gave him their tickets to the Opéra and the Comédie-Française.

"What's this?" Robin asked.

"Your farewell gift, Robin." Molly reached for his hand. "We'll be going back to Florence at the end of the week."

"Molly and I had a long discussion about our future when we went back to our hotel to change for dinner," Samuel added.

"You know that little gallery I talked about opening, Robin? Well, I'm finally going to do it."

"In America, of course," Robin said.

"Of course. With my husband." She blew Samuel a kiss. "In another year or so I would be too old for modeling, anyway. There's only one man I want to pose for now."

"I will miss you, *chérie*."

"We'll be back," Molly promised.

"Bring the children." Robin gave them both a sly grin.

After dinner, they bade Robin goodbye and returned to their hotel. Arm in arm, they stood beside their window and looked out over the city.

"I'm going to miss Paris," Samuel said.

"You definitely will not."

"I can see by that wicked smiled that you're up to something. Out with it, my sweet."

"The best part of Paris is going home with you. And I have every intention of seeing that you don't miss a single thrill."

"I like the sound of that." He pulled her close. "I've always wanted my own special Venus."

*   *   *   *   *

COMING NEXT MONTH

#736 VIRGIN TERRITORY—Suzanne Carey
A Diamond Jubilee Book!
Reporter Crista O'Malley had planned to change her status as "the last virgin in Chicago." But columnist Phil Catterini was determined to protect her virtue—and his bachelorhood! Could the two go hand in hand...into virgin territory?

#737 INVITATION TO A WEDDING—Helen R. Myers
All-business Blair Lawrence was in a bind. Desperate for an escort to her brother's wedding, she invited the charming man who watered her company's plants...never expecting love to bloom.

#738 PROMISE OF MARRIAGE—Kristina Logan
After being struck by Cupid's arrow—literally—divorce attorney Barrett Fox fell hard for beautiful Kate Marlowe. But he was a true cynic.... Could she convince him of the power of love?

#739 THROUGH THICK AND THIN—Anne Peters
Store owner Daniel Morgan had always been in control—until spunky security guard Lisa Hanrahan sent him head over heels. Now he needs to convince Lisa to guard his heart—forever.

#740 CIMARRON GLORY—Pepper Adams
Book II of *Cimarron Stories*
Stubborn Glory Roberts had her heart set on lassoing the elusive Ross Forbes. But would the rugged rancher's past keep them apart?

#741 CONNAL—Diana Palmer
Long, Tall Texans
Diana Palmer's fortieth Silhouette story is a delightful comedy of errors that resulted from a forgotten night—and a forgotten marriage—as Long, Tall Texan Connal Tremayne and Pepi Mathews battle over their past...and their future.

AVAILABLE THIS MONTH

#730 BORROWED BABY
Marie Ferrarella

#731 FULL BLOOM
Karen Leabo

#732 THAT MAN NEXT DOOR
Judith Bowen

#733 HOME FIRES BURNING BRIGHT
Laurie Paige

#734 BETTER TO HAVE LOVED
Linda Varner

#735 VENUS DE MOLLY
Peggy Webb

SILHOUETTE'S "BIG WIN"
SWEEPSTAKES RULES & REGULATIONS
NO PURCHASE NECESSARY TO ENTER OR RECEIVE A PRIZE

1. To enter and join the Reader Service, scratch off the metallic strips on all your BIG WIN tickets #1-#6. This will reveal the values for each sweepstakes entry number, the number of free book(s) you will receive, and your free bonus gift as part of our Reader Service. If you do not wish to take advantage of our Reader Service, but wish to enter the Sweepstakes only, scratch off the metallic strips on your BIG WIN tickets #1-#4. Return your entire sheet of tickets intact. Incomplete and/or inaccurate entries are ineligible for that section or sections of prizes. Not responsible for mutilated or unreadable entries or inadvertent printing errors. Mechanically reproduced entries are null and void.

2. Whether you take advantage of this offer or not, your Sweepstakes numbers will be compared against a list of winning numbers generated at random by the computer. In the event that all prizes are not claimed by March 31, 1992, a random drawing will be held from all qualified entries received from March 30, 1990 to March 31, 1992, to award all unclaimed prizes. All cash prizes (Grand to Sixth), will be mailed to the winners and are payable by cheque in U.S. funds. Seventh prize to be shipped to winners via third-class mail. These prizes are in addition to any free, surprise or mystery gifts that might be offered. Versions of this sweepstakes with different prizes of approximate equal value may appear in other mailings or at retail outlets by Torstar Corp. and its affiliates.

3. The following prizes are awarded in this sweepstakes: ★ Grand Prize (1) $1,000,000; First Prize (1) $35,000; Second Prize (1) $10,000; Third Prize (5) $5,000; Fourth Prize (10) $1,000; Fifth Prize (100) $250; Sixth Prize (2500) $10; ★ ★ Seventh Prize (6000) $12.95 ARV.

   ★ This Sweepstakes contains a Grand Prize offering of $1,000,000 annuity. Winner will receive $33,333.33 a year for 30 years without interest totalling $1,000,000.

   ★ ★ Seventh Prize: A fully illustrated hardcover book published by Torstar Corp. Approximate value of the book is $12.95.

   Entrants may cancel the Reader Service at any time without cost or obligation to buy (see details in center insert card).

4. This promotion is being conducted under the supervision of Marden-Kane, Inc., an independent judging organization. By entering this Sweepstakes, each entrant accepts and agrees to be bound by these rules and the decisions of the judges, which shall be final and binding. Odds of winning in the random drawing are dependent upon the total number of entries received. Taxes, if any, are the sole responsibility of the winners. Prizes are nontransferable. All entries must be received by no later than 12:00 NOON, on March 31, 1992. The drawing for all unclaimed sweepstakes prizes will take place May 30, 1992, at 12:00 NOON, at the offices of Marden-Kane, Inc., Lake Success, New York.

5. This offer is open to residents of the U.S., the United Kingdom, France and Canada, 18 years or older except employees and their immediate family members of Torstar Corp., its affiliates, subsidiaries, Marden-Kane, Inc., and all other agencies and persons connected with conducting this Sweepstakes. All Federal, State and local laws apply. Void wherever prohibited or restricted by law. Any litigation respecting the conduct and awarding of a prize in this publicity contest may be submitted to the Régie des loteries et courses du Québec.

6. Winners will be notified by mail and may be required to execute an affidavit of eligibility and release which must be returned within 14 days after notification or, an alternative winner will be selected. Canadian winners will be required to correctly answer an arithmetical skill-testing question administered by mail which must be returned within a limited time. Winners consent to the use of their names, photographs and/or likenesses for advertising and publicity in conjunction with this and similar promotions without additional compensation.

7. For a list of major winners, send a stamped, self-addressed envelope to: WINNERS LIST, c/o MARDEN-KANE, INC., P.O. BOX 701, SAYREVILLE, NJ 08871. Winners Lists will be fulfilled after the May 30, 1992 drawing date.

If Sweepstakes entry form is missing, please print your name and address on a 3" × 5" piece of plain paper and send to:

In the U.S.
Silhouette's "BIG WIN" Sweepstakes
901 Fuhrmann Blvd.
P.O. Box 1867
Buffalo, NY 14269-1867

In Canada
Silhouette's "BIG WIN" Sweepstakes
P.O. Box 609
Fort Erie, Ontario
L2A 5X3

Offer limited to one per household.
© 1989 Harlequin Enterprises Limited   Printed in the U.S.A.

LTY-S790RR

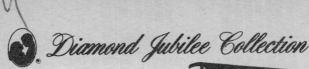

Diamond Jubilee Collection

It's our 10th Anniversary... and *you* get a present!

This collection of early Silhouette Romances features novels written by three of your favorite authors:

ANN MAJOR—*Wild Lady*
ANNETTE BROADRICK—*Circumstantial Evidence*
DIXIE BROWNING—*Island on the Hill*

* **These Silhouette Romance titles were first published in the early 1980s and have not been available since!**

* **Beautiful Collector's Edition bound in antique green simulated leather to last a lifetime!**

* **Embossed in gold on the cover and spine!**

--------✂ **PROOF OF PURCHASE**